He was a willing captive

"I told you this was my secret place, Kane. Now you're in my power." Rachel's voice was low and throaty, as mysterious as the shadows.

Kane kissed her neck, his lips tracing a path to her ear. "So? And what will you do with me?" he murmured.

"Does this mean you're surrendering?" She leaned away from him just enough to meet his slumberous gaze.

His teasing hand followed the swelling curve of her breast. "On one condition."

"No conditions! Surrender has to be absolute . . . complete."

With a sly grin, he pulled her back into his arms. "In that case, you've just met my terms. . . ."

Christine Rimmer says of her first kiss: "I remember the exact moment, what I was wearing—and that the boy was chewing Wrigley's spearmint gum." With such a romantic soul, and such a keen memory, Christine is a natural for writing romances. *The Road Home* is her first book, but she's devoted much of her time in the past to playwrighting. Christine lives in California with her husband, two cats and a dog named Amazing Grace.

The Road Home

CHRISTINE RIMMER

Harlequin Books

TORONTO • NEW YORK • LONDON
AMSTERDAM • PARIS • SYDNEY • HAMBURG
STOCKHOLM • ATHENS • TOKYO • MILAN

To Serita Stevens,
for her invaluable help and support,
and to Johnny,
who shall be forever young

Published May 1987

ISBN 0-373-25254-4

1

RACHEL STRETCHED, wriggling her toes in the sand. The smile of pure contentment she allowed herself curved her firm lips to a subtle sensuality. She felt the rays of the afternoon sun as an actual caress, a tracking of warm, invisible fingers along oil-shiny limbs. A few feet away the river made a hollow, beating question mark of sound as it tumbled down the rocks. Wind-stirred evergreens sighed in answer.

How many times—stuck in congested L.A. traffic, or battling with a recalcitrant client, or swimming in the chlorinated pool at her apartment—had she longed to be right here? She had promised herself this vacation in her beloved Sierra foothills for over a year now. Nothing—and no one—was going to take the savor out of it.

Lifting up on an elbow, she gazed across the crystal-line water to the jutting slate crags that gave this spot along the Yuba river its name: the Cliffs.

"My Cliffs," she said aloud, knowing that only willows and evergreens heard.

This had been her favorite place to come as a child and as an awkward, leggy adolescent. "Finding Rachel is never the problem," Gran used to say, peering over the top of her bifocals, dark eyes twinkling. "It merely takes a while to get to her." The Cliffs were difficult enough to reach that Rachel could usually be alone. And the beauty of them always soothed her whenever she was troubled.

The gentle wind toyed with the unruly masses of her cinnamon-shot brown hair. A random tendril kissed her cheek and caught between her lips. It was always like this when she let it hang free. Uncontrollable. She took a brush and a rubber band from her bag and coaxed the thick coils into a high ponytail.

Rising, she went to the river's edge. The clear, green water was cold enough this early in summer to elicit a gasp. She got in quickly, ducking her head beneath the surface, swimming underwater, floating up to breathe halfway across. Her clean, even strokes took her to the other side, where she pulled herself up onto the rocks. The heat of the afternoon sun on her river-cold skin was a tangible joy.

Rachel sat down on a small ledge and gathered her long legs into her chest. She would soon be dry and ready to swim back to the beach. Shrugging the single strap of her white Kamali suit off her left shoulder, she let the sun have the whole of her back.

It was then, when she gazed back the way she'd come, over the bright water that caught and reflected the gold luminescence in her almond-brown eyes, that she saw him. Kane.

He stood at the edge of the trees, half in shadow, arms across his powerful chest, the side of his face that was in the light, gleaming bronze under the raw honey of his hair. For a suspended moment their eyes locked.

It seemed as if, even across the cold slash of the current, she melted into him. Kane. She could almost feel his muscular arms closing around her. Could almost taste again the sweet and salt of him, smell the woodsy scent that only came from him, hear the deep-timbered baritone of his voice demanding all of her.

Six years, and she still wanted him.

She was a fool. She shook her head briskly, the wet shock of her ponytail whipping across her face. How dared he come here? How long had he watched her?

In one fluid motion, Rachel got to her feet. Swiftly pulling the strap of her suit back in place, she set her shoulders squarely and dropped her hands to her sides. Her brown and gold eyes, all softness gone now, leveled a command at him: *Go away. You have no right to be here.*

Kane smiled, that lazy grin of his. Even across the river she could see the stubborn set to his jaw. He wasn't going anywhere. He came out of the half shadow and into the light, taking the beach in smooth, loose-jointed strides. He wore loose khakis and a pair of lace-up boots. The rock-hard planes of his chest stood out in sharp relief, tapering down to a tight waist. She wanted to throw back her head and scream at him, "Why have you come here? This is my home!"

He sat down on a rock near her towel and unlaced his boots, pulling them off, then his socks, which he rolled up neatly and stuck inside the boots. He stood up again, unzipping his pants and stepping out of them.

At least he had the decency to wear swim trunks, Rachel thought, but the lithe power in his strong legs was not lost on her. That combination of strength and flexibility had always set him apart from other men—the sense that he would land on his feet even if pushed from a great height.

Damn him. He was coming the rest of the way to the water now. At the edge he stopped, meeting her hard gaze and matching it.

"Hello, Rachel," he said. His voice was low, but still she heard it.

Breaking the hold of his eyes, she dove, a shallow, perfect dive, cutting into the river with barely a splash. She swam straight for him in her even crawl. When her feet touched solid ground, she waded through the shallow water and up onto the beach.

"I said hello, Rachel."

She brushed past him and went to her towel. Grabbing her tennis shoes, she shoved them on her feet, wet sand and all, lacing them quickly. She crammed her arms into the sleeves of her white gauze shirt, almost tearing it, then tied the shirttails in a tight knot at her waist. Shaking out her white duck shorts, she stepped into them, yanking the zipper up with so much force that it stuck. Enraged, she pulled at it harder, only managing to lodge the flap more securely in the zipper teeth.

"Need some help?"

She could hear the barely controlled laughter in his voice. She could have killed him.

"The day I need your help, Kane Walker, is the day they lay me in the ground."

He cleared the distance between them and reached for her struggling hands.

"Easy. You'll break the teeth."

Rachel froze at his touch. The scent of him was as she remembered: man sweat and pine. Not wanting to, she lifted her head, took the force of his eyes full on, brown-laced eyes of smoky quartz. At five-eleven in her bare feet she was almost his height, and the bronze planes of his face were alarmingly near....

"Please, Kane." Her voice came out in a quavering whisper, belying the rage she wanted to feel.

"Please what?" His fine, long-fingered hands enclosed hers, sending little shivers along her arms that somehow felt like flame. She pulled her hands away. He let them go with a rueful slowness.

"You . . . you followed me."

"You've been avoiding me, as usual." Before she could protest, he grasped the zipper tab and dislodged it from the cloth. "There."

This close, she could see the little changes years can make: the tiny crow's-feet at the corners of his eyes; the faint lines like parentheses at the sides of his mouth; the barely detectable acne scars that had faded even more, as if what must have been a torment in his adolescence had only added to the rugged strength of the man he'd become.

Stifling the urge to touch the sandpaper cheek, Rachel lowered her eyes. They fell upon the long-fingered hands and the beaten silver ring with the almost-black stone in it.

"I still wear it." Kane's low voice was soft.

The dark stone glinted in the sunlight. Rachel wondered if he'd read her mind. She really had to get away from him.

"You're standing on my towel."

Kane stepped back. She grabbed the corners of the towel and shook the sand from it. Rolling it up quickly, she laid it across the top of her bag.

"No need to rush off. This beach is big enough for two."

She knew he was laughing at her again. She could see the flicker of amusement deepening the tiny lines around his eyes.

"Stop laughing," she snapped.

"Laughing? Who's laughing?" His face took on a mock-innocent air, but he couldn't quite control the twitch at the corner of his mouth. "Just being neighborly."

"You had no right to come here!" Rachel flung the words at him.

Kane's expression hardened. "I didn't know you owned this beach. I don't see your name on it."

"I'm not talking about the beach."

"Oh, I know," he taunted. "If you had your way, there'd be signs posted from Sacramento clear to Reno— and every one of them would say, Kane Walker, Keep Out!"

"Don't be ridiculous! I don't care where you go as long as I don't have to be there. I just want you to stay away from me. Is that so much to ask?"

"Rachel..." He took a step toward her again; she jerked back. "I told you once that someday I'd build a cabin in these mountains. You didn't seem to think it was such a bad idea then." His eyes searched her face, daring her to remember.

Gripping her bag against her breasts, Rachel widened her stance, seeking an anchor against the fluctuating tide of her emotions. The first time she'd been alone with him in six years, and it had to be here. At the Cliffs.

Was he thinking of the day they'd come here together? Of that secret place she knew inside one of the willow stands that rimmed the beach? Of their wet and gleaming bodies moving as one, his warm breath on her face, the strength of him surrounding her among the waving stalks?

Her mouth felt dry. She swallowed, moistening her upper lip with the tip of her tongue. He was staring at her, his own lips slightly parted now. From the core of her being she sensed exactly what was in his mind.

But that was the past. The dead and finished past. All she wanted from him now was to be left alone.

Rachel slung the bag over her shoulder. "Things were different then." Her shrug of denial was cool. Detached. She watched with satisfaction as his hands tightened into fists, noticed the effort it took him to make them go lax again.

"You mean that then you called the shots." One side of his sensual mouth curled upward. "You always did like calling the shots." He was baiting her again.

"What I like is no concern of yours."

He sighed and raked a hand back through his hair. "All right." His glance scanned the hills around them and came back to rest on her.

"This is not L.A., Rachel. It's going to become embarrassing for both of us if you duck into a shop whenever you see me coming down the street."

"I never—"

"You did. Last October. Melrose Avenue, wasn't it? In front of Fred Segal. You flew through that door so fast, I was surprised you didn't break the glass."

In spite of her tan, Rachel felt her skin reddening. She opened her mouth to protest again, but he gave her no chance.

"As I was saying, this isn't L.A. And if we're both here at the same time, we're going to run into each other. I suggest you learn to deal with it."

"You—you suggest . . ." she stammered, fuming at his arrogance.

"You heard what I said."

She was losing ground. That day on Melrose Avenue, she'd been sure he hadn't spotted her. And today she'd been determined not even to speak to him. Yet here they were, trading jabs like a pair of veteran boxers. The only intelligent move now was to leave before she lost her temper completely.

"You're right." She granted him a frosty smile. He'd see she knew how to deal with him. "You've got everything you ever wanted now, and I wish you all the pleasure you deserve from it." She turned to go.

Kane grabbed her arm. "You never believed I'd manage it." Accusing eyes bored into her. "You . . . indulged my fantasies that summer you brought me here, because you were sure I'd never actually be able to afford a place in your precious mountains."

"You're hurting my arm." Her tone was level. By physically detaining her, he had given her control. Kane winced as if she'd struck him; his cruel grip on her forearm abruptly loosened. She shook him off like a cobweb and walked away.

"Your grandmother invited me to the wedding," he said to her retreating back. "You be sure to tell her I'll be there."

Rachel pretended not to hear him as she made it to the cover of the trees and set her feet firmly on the deer trail that wound up the hill above the river.

By the time she'd showered and changed into dry jeans and a bright yellow cotton shirt, Rachel's anger had cooled somewhat. She really couldn't understand why she let Kane upset her so. What had been between them was long over, she reminded herself, and his motivation for building a vacation home up Goodyears Creek Road was none of her concern. Grudgingly she admitted to herself that his accusations had the ring of truth.

Seven years ago he'd been a part-time aerobics instructor who made his real living slinging pizzas at a small Italian restaurant near the boulevard. She *had* been sure then that he would never amount to much. Hollywood was full of guys like Kane had been, young and attractive, carrying a beat-up old Gibson guitar, dreaming of a future as a rock star and working as a waiter until the big break came.

Rachel had known the first time she'd gazed into those near-black eyes he was dangerous. She wasn't the only woman who would feel the almost electric charge that vibrated through him. But she'd been so young then, only twenty-two. And madly, dizzyingly in love for the first time. It had taken her a full year to face what he was. She had been hurt badly. There was no way she would ever let that happen again.

A big bumblebee teased lazily at the wild sweet peas that climbed the railing of the side porch, and Rachel drank in the restful quiet of late afternoon. Nat, Gran's black and white Australian sheepdog, snoozed at her feet.

Across the street, a clever ray of sun slipped between thick cedar branches and hit the windows of the old schoolhouse. Gran had taught there long ago. But for the past thirty years school-age children had been bused to Downieville, four miles to the northeast on Highway 49. Now the schoolhouse was the community center for the small town of Goodyears Bar.

The side door opened, and Gran came out to join her, carrying two iced teas garnished with sprigs of fresh bergamot, a wild, mintlike herb that grew at the edges of her garden.

"I thought you might appreciate a cool drink." Gran's crisp schoolteacher diction was softened by the slight quaver of age. "Did you enjoy your swim, dear?" She lowered herself carefully into the folding chair next to Rachel.

"Kane Walker was there." Rachel took the cool glass from her grandmother's outstretched hand.

"Such a nice young man. Did you know he made a very generous donation to the community fund? Now it appears we'll be able to replace the schoolhouse roof, after all."

"He said you invited him to the wedding."

Gran's dark eyes glinted teasingly, enlarged by the lenses of her bifocals. She smiled, and a network of wrinkles spread like rays across the strong-boned face. She took a sip from her glass.

"Ah. So refreshing. Do taste it, dear. I've put a small spoon of honey in yours. I know you like the sweetness."

Rachel lifted the glass to her lips. "Just right," she said, and leaned back.

"You reminded me of your mother, sitting out here. I glanced through the kitchen window and..." A resigned sigh escaped Gran's lips. "You have her hair, dear. And often that same faraway look about the eyes."

"Lydia's eyes were more green, weren't they?" Rachel felt uncomfortable when anyone compared her to Lydia. She considered herself more a daughter to the woman sitting next to her than to the strange, complex creature who had died when Rachel was ten.

"Yes. Her eyes were green," Gran replied after a moment. "Both she and Janice inherited your grandfather's eyes. Unfortunately, they had little else in common. Janice has always taken life in stride, while your mother—"

"Is Aunt Jannie going to make it to the wedding?" Rachel knew she was interrupting, but she didn't want to dwell on thoughts of Lydia. Her memories of the woman who had given her birth always produced a sharp ache somewhere in the vicinity of her heart.

"Janice will be here," Gran answered softly. "She and Miles are flying into Sacramento a few days before. Chris will pick them up, and they'll stay at his house."

"I've been thinking about the wedding party." Rachel poked at an ice cube, submerging it and watching it pop to the surface again. "I wish you'd at least let me do some centerpieces for the tables."

"Always the decorator." Gran laughed.

"Not decorator. Designer. Party designer," Rachel corrected with good-humored patience.

"We'll keep it simple. That's how both Gideon and I prefer it." Gran's tone was gentle but firm. "You know I'm proud of you. You've made a profitable career doing what you love best. But you've come to Goodyears to relax. And I intend to see you do just that."

"It's not every day my grandmother gets married," Rachel protested. "I want to—"

"There'll be plenty to do without your worrying about the flowers."

Rachel couldn't suppress a smile at this last. Despite her seventy-nine years, Ethel Neal Carver was every bit the schoolteacher at heart, loving nothing so much as creating projects and enlisting the aid of all and sundry in their accomplishment. Still, Rachel intended to contribute, despite Gran's objections. But there was no sense in arguing now. Rachel had her plans, and she would just let them unfold when the time came.

"I am a little concerned, however, about the problem of closet space."

Rachel shot Gran a puzzled look. What did closet space have to do with the wedding?

"Gideon will be moving in here after our honeymoon," Gran explained. "The upstairs closet is full of your mother's things. Janice and I packed them away right after Lydia died. There never seemed to be a reason to go through them again. But now . . ."

"Do you want me to help you?"

"Oh, Rachel, dear. Would you?"

Rachel nodded. Her grandmother's capable old hand came across the distance between them and patted her arm.

"I thought we could decide on the things we want to save and give the rest to the Community Club for the next rummage sale."

"Sounds like a plan." Rachel sighed and got to her feet. She should have helped Gran clear out all that junk years ago.

"WHAT SHALL WE DO with all these catalogs?" Gran smoothed a stray wisp of hair away from her forehead.

The contents of the upstairs closet were spread on the floor and across the twin beds that snuggled under the eaves.

"Throw them out?" Rachel suggested hopefully, all too aware of how Gran hated waste.

Lydia had been something of an amateur naturalist, her unfulfilled dreams centering on vague plans to escape forever into the wilds. She would spend hours going through the catalogs from Sears and Montgomery Ward, circling the pictures of down sleeping bags and Coleman stoves that she might need on her travels.

"I could use them to start the kindling," Gran went on, ignoring Rachel's much simpler solution.

"Gran. You've got stacks of old newspapers cluttering up the service porch already."

"This paper should be recycled."

"It'll be recycled, all right," Rachel said. "Chris will take it all to the dump for you, where it will eventually decompose, providing fertilizer for the forests of the future."

"It's not fair to ask Chris. He's always doing little favors for me. I feel as if I'm taking advantage of him."

"What else is a grandson for?"

Gran chuckled. "I have no idea where you inherited that stubborn streak. Very well. Fertilizer for the forests of the future, it is." Together they stacked the dog-eared wishbooks at the top of the stairs.

"Now. As for the antique bottle collection . . ." Gran clapped her hands, ridding them of dust from the catalogs.

Rachel picked up a glass container at random from the overflowing cardboard box.

"Priceless." She wrinkled her patrician nose in a characteristic gesture that made her fine-boned face look almost cute. "Authentic Old Turkey from the look of it."

Gran cast her a chiding glance. After all, these old bottles found at deserted campsites and around the gold mines that dotted the surrounding hills had been just that, priceless, to Lydia.

"I suppose some of them might be valuable," Rachel conceded, her voice softening. She hadn't meant to make fun of Lydia. It just seemed important to keep the tone light. "Why don't we hold on to a few that appeal to us and give the rest to the rummage sale?"

"Oh, look at this." Gran lifted a single snapshot from another of the dusty boxes. "The day they went off to Reno to be married." The dark eyes were misty as she looked at Rachel. "I had no idea this was here."

"Ahooga! Ahooga!" The blare of an ancient car horn resounded from the street below.

Rachel felt a surge of gratitude at the timely interruption. "The eager bridegroom has arrived," she commented dryly.

"He never did bother to call first," Gran mumbled. Setting the tattered photograph on the chipped maple bed table, Gran lifted her hands to smooth back her hair, tucking a few almost-white strands back into the corona of French braids. "I must look a mess."

"Nonsense," Rachel said curtly, suddenly feeling older than this bride-to-be of seventy-nine who stood beside her. "You look . . . like a woman in love."

Gran glanced at her reflection in the faded glass above a pasteboard bookcase.

"Yes. Yes, I suppose I do." There was pride in the statement, and not a little wonder.

"Ahooga!" The old horn sounded again.

"Hold your horses," Gran said under her breath. "I may be a woman in love, but it takes me a minute to get down the stairs these days."

Rachel watched from a dormer window as her grandmother went out to meet the tall, thin man who unfolded himself from the wheezing Model A. He doffed his battered baseball cap with a flourish when Gran approached him, then pulled her into the circle of his unbelievably long arms.

Rachel smiled down at them. Gideon Gentry reminded her of some wiry, awkward old bird of prey. The way his gray hair had thinned back from his temples, making the hawklike nose seem to leap out from his face, only enhanced the impression. "An eagle with glasses," Rachel said to herself as the thick lenses caught the light.

Gran looked up at the window where Rachel stood watching and signaled for her to come down.

"Gideon insists that we're going out to dinner and then to the movies," Gran called as Rachel ran down the porch steps. It was necessary for Gran to raise her voice to compete with the rattling sputters that issued from beneath the hood of Gideon's ancient car. "Gideon, can't you turn that thing off?"

"Nope." His lopsided grin was not in the least apologetic. "Might never get her started again if I do that." He turned to Rachel. "Put on your glad rags, gal. We're goin' out to paint the town."

"All the way to Downieville. In that?" Rachel rolled her eyes heavenward.

"I like 'em mature. No need to break 'em in that way." Gideon patted the shuddering hood affectionately.

"Gideon, please!" When Gran's voice got that edge to it, even Gideon knew she meant business. Relenting, he pulled the key from the ignition. The old car shook and clattered a few more times, then was still. "Now come inside while we get cleaned up."

A half hour later, freshly showered and dressed in her polyester culottes and a white eyelette blouse, smelling discreetly of lavender, Gran climbed into the Model A next to Gideon, and the two of them sputtered off for their night on the town. It had taken some convincing, but Rachel had finally assured her grandmother that she didn't mind staying home by herself.

Nat whined a little as Gran drove away. He didn't like to be left alone. Rachel stroked the dog's head affectionately.

"Hey, boy. What about me? I'm still here." The dog looked up at her with soulful eyes. "You can come inside and help me finish upstairs," she promised. Nat wagged his tail and followed her back into the house.

Long shadows had claimed the surrounding hills, and dark was near by the time Rachel finished dividing Lydia's belongings into neat piles. In the end she had managed to narrow down the "save" pile to two large boxes. It had all gone quite smoothly without Gran there to fret over every discard.

She had kept the leather-bound copies of three Conrad Richter novels, *The Trees, The Fields* and *The Town*, as well as the many well-used volumes on wildlife and herbal remedies. It had also seemed a good idea to save the old Downieville High School yearbooks, her mother's diploma and the blue books full of essays scrawled in Lydia's impatient hand.

Rachel chose several of the least damaged bottles. Some of them even looked as if they might be pretty when she had a chance to clean them up. Rachel had heard somewhere that cobalt glass was prized now by collectors, and a few of the perfume bottles were milk glass—cloudy white. They probably weren't that old, she reminded herself, but she kept them, anyway.

Lydia's clothes were no problem; tattered jeans and shirts would go to the rummage sale. Lydia had rarely been seen in dresses, preferring sturdy men's pants, flannel shirts and the freedom that went with them.

Rachel wondered who had taken the wedding snapshot. Probably Gran. A tall woman, her dark hair pulled severely back from her head, stood in Gran's front yard. She wore what appeared to be a new coat with a fur collar. She was squinting into the harsh winter sun, her long legs in unaccustomed high heels held stiffly, close together. Beside the woman, a man in an expensive gray pinstripe suit and trench coat had thrown a possessive arm around her shoulders. Though the sun must have been in his eyes, he did not squint. Rather his gaze was level, self-assured: a man used to taking what he wanted.

The photograph had been folded in the middle. A line ran down between the two figures but could not separate them; they were too close together. Rachel resisted the urge to tear the thing in half and consign it to the wood-burning side of the big gas stove. Gran would never forgive her. She slipped the photo inside the cover of one of Gran's photo albums.

After a dinner of cold chicken and fresh zucchini from the garden, she went outside to watch the evening primroses bloom. When they were children she and her cousin, Chris, used to sit out here often. They would watch in quiet wonder as the trees became friendly monsters and the yellow flowers opened so fast that you could see it happening, like time-lapse photography, when night took all the world.

She had sat here with Kane, too, that summer when it had seemed as if the love she felt could make anything right. They had held hands like school kids while she'd pointed out the constellations, so bright against the indigo Sierra sky.

"Someday I'll have a place up here." He had squeezed her hand. "Will you share it with me, Rachel?"

Rachel had leaned against him then, surrendering to the familiar, licking warmth that always moved inside her at his nearness. "Oh, yes. You know I will," she had whispered, knowing that would never happen, thinking of the primroses—opening—spreading willing petals to embrace the night.

His strong arms had come around her. The fresh, sharp scent of him had seemed like the pines and mountain streams made flesh. His mouth came down to drink from hers, his tongue probing, seeking, finding the core of heat and need, stoking the banked fires to flame. His hand strayed up, palm flat against her breast, rubbing lightly, bringing the nipple to surging life through the cotton fabric of her shirt.

"Tonight," he growled low against her ear.

"After Gran goes to sleep...." The pounding of her blood was like the river in swift places, tumbling fast and hard....

Beside her on the porch, Nat whimpered. Must be a bad dream....

Rachel came back from the past as from under an anesthetic. The dog rolled over, and she scratched the soft hair of his belly.

It must have been the memories stirred up by going through Lydia's things that had made her think of Kane again. Well, she wasn't like Lydia, a wild woods creature with no resources, nothing to fall back on when a good-looking, sophisticated man had come to claim her.

Rachel knew Kane Walker for what he was, a man who, in the end, had opted for success at any price. A man who had sold himself to another woman when that woman had offered him financial backing to open his own business. Getting too close to a man like that meant heartbreak. Rachel would never pay that price again.

2

THE FOURTH OF JULY dawned clear and bright. Awakened early by the insistent chattering of a blue jay outside the window near her bed, Rachel pressed her nose against the screen.

"All right, all right. I hear you," she scolded back. The bird cocked his head to the side, squawked at her once more for good measure and flew off up the hill above the flume.

Downstairs Gran was already moving about, probably hoping Rachel would get up soon so she could turn up the volume on the morning news. Stretching lustily, Rachel swung her bare feet to the floor.

The Fourth was a big day in Downieville, and Rachel was looking forward to it with the anticipation of an overgrown child. There would be breakfast at the Quartz Café with her cousin, Chris, and his family; the races in the afternoon; the Fireman's Ball that night.

"A three-letter word for a chicken preceder or follower. Any ideas, dear?" Gran looked up from her crossword puzzle as Rachel made her way to the coffee pot.

"You're ten times better at those things than anybody else. How should I know?" Rachel stirred two spoons of sugar into the rich black brew. "You can turn up the TV now. I'm awake."

"Oh, no. I can't think if it's too loud. How about a four-letter word for burly bovines?"

"Sorry." Rachel shrugged and sipped at her coffee. "Coming with us for breakfast?"

"I've already eaten, dear." Gran's lips had pursed to that wrinkled little bow that meant she was trying to concentrate and she wished no one would ask her another question.

"Suit yourself. Can I use the shower now?"

"I don't know if you *can* but you *may*."

The clear water hit Rachel on the chest, cascading like the joining tributaries of a river in the valley between her breasts, over the flat plane of her stomach and down her long legs to the tub drain at her feet. There had been a time when the shower nozzle was way over her head, but now she had to duck to rinse her hair. The little window over the tub, which looked out on the pump house and the open wooden flume bearing the town's water supply, was now the same height as her chest.

Careful not to use all the hot water, Rachel finished off with cold. She gasped when the spray turned icy, hearing the pump outside knock a few more times and switch off. After drying herself briskly with one of her grandmother's flowered towels, she went upstairs to dress in red shorts and a striped red, white and blue top, feeling her choice of colors was quite in keeping with the spirit of the day.

Rachel drove her cream-white Mercedes 450SL up to Downieville. The car was her one true extravagance so far, bought last January after the most successful holiday season she'd ever had.

"Most successful *so far*," she reminded herself as she slipped a tape on the deck.

Rolling the window down, she let the wind have its way with her hair. Tapping rhythm on the steering wheel, she was careful to watch her speed. Though she knew every turn of this four-mile drive, she was in no hurry. Besides, it was a long drop to the river on her right.

For the fun of it she stopped at the little café and gift shop at Coyoteville Cabins and bought three T-shirts, all in different colors. One for Chris, one for his wife, Sarah, and a child's version for Johnny. Rachel realized that Sarah probably wouldn't get much use out of hers until next year; she was due to have a second child in October. But she knew Chris's petite, curly headed wife would appreciate the thought.

Just as Rachel returned to her car and was tossing the gifts in the back seat, a moss-green Land Rover drove by. Kane's. She looked up in time to catch his burning glance as it swept down from the tousled masses of her hair to the tips of her red canvas shoes. Rachel found herself staring back, nonplussed by the dropping sensation in the pit of her stomach.

In that instant he was gone, rounding the bend toward Cannon Point. Frustration welled up inside her. She got in the car quickly, slamming the door, gripping the smooth wood steering wheel as if she would strangle it. Damn the man! How was she supposed to get him off her mind when he kept popping up every time she turned around?

The perfectly tuned engine of her car rolled over and purred like a cat when she twisted the key. Leave it to Kane to drive a beat up old four-wheel-drive Land Rover, even now that he could afford the best. She wondered vaguely if he still owned that disgraceful wreck of a Buick that he had always claimed was a classic. She wouldn't put it past him. He never had had much appreciation for the finer things in life. Rachel shifted the sleek Mercedes into gear and headed toward Downieville.

Smokey the Bear pointed a shovel at the word High on the fire-danger sign at the entrance to town. It was early in the year for such a warning, but Rachel knew fire and flood were always major threats to this small mountain community built at the place where the North Yuba and Downie rivers converged. The evergreens and live oaks that surrounded the town were a tall, rolling carpet of green dotted here and there with houses and divided at low ground by two rivers meeting, becoming one.

Flags and patriotic bunting were strung from post to post over the wooden sidewalks along Main Street, and the big parking lot in the flat between the Quartz Café and the gas station was already almost full. Makeshift booths had been set up in the empty space where the St. Charles Hotel had stood before the fire of 1947. The shiny red community fire truck was parked sideways at the junction of Main and Commercial. The cleared space would be used for the coming races.

Rachel picked out a few familiar faces among the many tourists and prospectors who had turned out for the festivities. Some didn't recognize the dark-haired woman in the fancy car, but others waved and smiled, and she returned their greetings.

Making a right on Commercial Street and crossing the bridge, she was relieved to find a parking space a little beyond Chris's house. Chris and his family were waiting on the porch when she came through the gate.

"Gettin' better lookin' every year, String Bean," Chris announced in his gravelly drawl, wrapping Rachel in a bear hug.

"What is that growing on your face?" Rachel asked, wrinkling her nose as she reached up to tug at his shaggy red beard.

"Never trust a man with a beard." Sarah laughed. She lifted her small body, grown heavy with advancing pregnancy, from the porch swing and reached out for a hug of her own.

"Cousin Rache, Cousin Rache!" Johnny waved his chubby arms at her, and Rachel scooped him up and deposited a kiss on his cheek. He immediately squirmed away. Johnny was five now. Kisses were for kids.

They walked across the bridge together, Johnny clutching Rachel's finger in his fist. He had insisted on changing into the T-shirt she'd bought him, which was just a bit snug.

"See how big I got? You're big, too, Cousin Rache. But not as big as Daddy." Rachel heard the snort behind her and knew Chris was trying to keep his laughter under control. "You better get married now, Cousin Rache. You can have a baby then, just like Mommy."

The blue eyes so much like his mother's regarded her seriously. Rachel smiled down at him, knowing enough about children not to argue. Few people were harder to convince than a five-year-old who had made up his mind.

The Quartz Café was crowded. It had taken fifteen minutes to get a seat in one of the booths that lined the walls. Rachel spent the time reacquainting herself with the changes in the place. The long counter with the padded stools was gone, and the wood paneling made the room seem smaller somehow. But it was still the Quartz, where she and Chris used to come dripping wet in their swimsuits and order cherry colas. Where they would spin on the stools and make faces at themselves in the mirrored wall that had run behind the soda fountain, discussing their plans to go frog hunting or into business for themselves, selling hellgrammites in bandage cans to fishermen for bait.

The food was plain coffee-shop fare, eggs, hash browns and bacon. They were sipping a last cup of coffee companionably while Sarah patiently explained to Johnny that he was still a little young for coffee himself, when Chris's broad face broke into a friendly grin.

"Hiya, Kane. How's it goin'?"

He was standing right beside her. The bustle in the busy restaurant had covered his entrance, and Rachel's back was to the door.

"Fine, Chris." The warm rumble of his voice licked along her nerves.

The two men shook hands. Sarah beamed up at him. Johnny studied him gravely over a half-chewed gob of blueberry muffin.

"You remember Rachel?" Chris asked, all innocence.

Rachel almost kicked her cousin under the table, but she smiled politely up at Kane. The teasing light in the brown-black eyes was not lost on her.

"How are you, Rachel? It's good to see you again." Couldn't everyone see the man was baiting her?

He wore running shoes and Adidas shorts, blue with white piping. The springy hairs along his infuriating legs had a dusty bronze sheen, even in the dimmer indoor light. She knew how tawny hairs much the same spread across the chest beneath the crew-neck shirt, forming a tantalizing V that dipped down along the corded firmness of his belly. Rachel hung on to her coffee cup for dear life.

"Nice to see you, Kane," she said in a voice dripping with artificial sweetener.

Chris insisted that Kane pull up a chair. Rachel tried to sort out the tangle of her emotions as they discussed the terrific turnout for the races, the shiny-new paint job on the community fire truck and the trees Kane planned to thin out on his property. It was only neighborly that Chris would offer to help and that Kane would return the kindness by promising Rachel's cousin a share of the wood.

Rachel was careful to appear friendly, answering briefly when a question was asked of her. Once a naked, hair-roughened knee brushed hers under the table. Though a lovely flush deepened the sun-kissed gold of her skin, Rachel didn't jerk away, but raised her leg casually and crossed it over the other one.

They left Kane at last, waiting for his cheese omelet, his thick gold hair falling across his forehead as he and Chris shook hands again.

"See you later, Rachel." Kane's tone was casual, but she knew he was waiting for her to say something challenging in return.

"Goodbye, Kane." She ignored the way his eyes caressed the satin length of her legs when she slipped from the booth and stood above him. She always felt more in control when she was looking down. Smiling distantly, she followed the others out the door and into the busy street.

The races didn't start until two, so they went back to Chris's for a while and sat on the porch, catching up on events since Rachel had last been with them, calling greetings to familiar passersby on the sidewalk beyond the gate.

AT ONE O'CLOCK, agreeing to return for them in an hour, Rachel crossed the bridge again to join in the carefree spirit of the holiday crowds. She strolled up one side of

Main Street and down the other, enduring the good-natured jostling of tourists in a hurry to have fun.

Feeling expansive, she bought three tickets from the Mountain Star Quilters though she knew she wouldn't be there for the draw in September. At the table set up for the Cemetery Restoration Fund, she spent twenty dollars on a set of pot holders and dish towels printed with little rhymes. Each one was bordered with grinning cartoon insects: giggling bees, chortling dragonflies. Of course, she knew how silly they would look in the gleaming spareness of her blue-tiled kitchen in L.A., but it was for a good cause.

The Forest Service had a large booth in the St. Charles flat across from the movie house. She was looking over the posters of trees and wildlife when a balloon fight erupted in the street behind her. Before it was over, several of the water-filled missiles had exploded on contact. A large green one hit the pavement at Rachel's feet, drenching her canvas shoes and splattering her legs.

The ranger in the booth, who looked to be all of eighteen, clucked sympathetically. "Happens every holiday, ma'am. But it's only water." He produced a roll of paper towels. "I try to be prepared," he added with modest nonchalance.

"Thanks." Rachel tore off a few sheets and passed the roll to a plump lady in a pink muumuu who had also been doused. Then she bent to wipe the water off herself.

Crouched amid a forest of milling legs and feet, Rachel caught a glimpse of blue running shoes. Her own soggy feet forgotten, she gazed up two well-shaped calves, along muscled thighs to a pair of Adidas shorts. Rising, she tossed the rumpled towel into a nearby trash can.

Kane wasn't more than fifteen feet away, engaged in a transaction with a balding peddler of costume jewelry.

"Terrific," she muttered to no one in particular.

"'Scuse me?" asked the ranger who had given her the towel.

"These..." She gestured vaguely at the posters. "They're terrific."

"Which one's your favorite?"

In her peripheral vision she watched the jewelry seller hand Kane a small box. Who was he buying jewelry for?

"Er... miss?"

Rachel arranged her face into an enthusiastic smile. "All of them. I really just... I like them all!"

"Then take one of each. Compliments of the Forest Service."

"Oh, I couldn't...." Just what she needed. Six twenty-by-thirty posters of indigenous flora and fauna.

"They're free," was the coaxing reply.

Kane had paid for the box and turned in her direction. Brown-threaded black eyes were focused on her. The pleasant afternoon seemed suddenly too warm. Rachel stiffened her spine. If his presence raised her temperature, from now on he wasn't going to know it.

The young man was leaning across the booth now, lowering his voice. "I'm supposed to make sure they're all gone by five when we shut down."

"Well, in that case." She granted him a thousand-watt smile. "I guess I'll have to take one of each."

Reddening to his hairline, the youth passed her six rolled tubes, which she lodged under her free arm.

The lady in the muumuu chose three posters for herself and moved on to the jewelry peddler. Kane took the empty space.

"Choose a poster, Kane. They're free." Rachel's voice was satisfyingly level.

Her admirer in the booth cleared his throat and retreated to a folding chair. "Yeah. Help yourself."

"Maybe later." The husky drawl was accompanied by a casual shrug.

"Did you find anything you liked?" she asked inanely, indicating the bags he carried with a tilt of her head, intent on keeping things completely innocuous.

He blinked once, as if her lack of hostility had caught him off guard. "Just souvenirs. For the folks. Some earrings for Vicky."

"Vicky?" The name was vaguely familiar.

"Mariette's daughter."

Rachel's smile felt pasted on her face. Mariette was the woman with whom Kane had betrayed her.

"Vicky," she echoed over brightly. "I remember Vicky as all eyes and long black hair. She liked to sing, didn't she?"

Kane nodded. "She still does."

"Pardon me, folks." A burly man nudged between them and grabbed a poster. Kane's eyes stayed locked on her face, daring her to say a single word against dear little Vicky's adulterous mother. Rachel had no intention of falling prey to such a challenge.

The loudspeaker came on again. Ten minutes until the races.

"Well, I'd better get these back to the car." Rachel clutched the posters more tightly, hefting the bag with the towels and pot holders. "Be seeing you."

"You sure you can manage all that by yourself?" He cocked an eyebrow at her full arms. That lazy grin was back on his face.

"I'm sure," she confirmed too quickly, already turning and heading for the bridge.

Her wet shoes made faint squishing sounds with each step. She thought she heard a muffled chuckle behind her.

"Wonderful," she mumbled grimly. Her first real vacation in two years, and she was doomed to spend it figuring out ways to keep her blood pressure down.

Still, she'd handled herself pretty well in the restaurant, as well as just now. All she had to do was keep things light. And brief. That way dangerous emotions would not have a chance to flare up between them.

"Cousin Rache, hurry up! We're almost late!" Johnny jumped up and down beyond the gate to Chris's house. Rachel hurried to her car, unloaded her purchases and joined the little boy and his parents as they came out onto the sidewalk.

Johnny won the preschoolers race, barely beating a freckle-faced, towheaded boy who stumbled along beside him for most of the way. The silver-dollar prize looked like a king's ransom in his plump fist. He vowed to save it and be rich when he grew up.

Then there were the bag races and the one in which the contestants had to carry a potato on a spoon. Next came the log-sawing and dirt-digging contests, skills much prized by loggers and miners respectively.

Rachel was breathing a sigh of relief that she had seen the last of Kane for the day when he appeared for the adult males hundred-yard dash. He won easily. A ghost of a smile haunted her lips when she saw him run. It had always seemed as if he were actually claiming the ground beneath his feet with his fluid, even stride. They used to run together often when— She pulled her thoughts up short.

"New in town," commented a voice behind her. It belonged to one of the old-timers who liked to sit on the benches in front of the Downieville Grocery, swapping tales of the good old days when the rivers ran with gold and all the nuggets were the size of your fist. "Rich," the man went on. "Owns a bunch of them fancy health spas down Los Angeles way. But don't let them new tennis shoes fool you," he informed his similarly grizzled companion. "That guy's okay. Stops by the store lots of times and listens real careful when I tell him 'bout how things used to be. That's a guy as got a sense of history, a guy as wants to hear the truth from them that knows."

Without thinking Rachel turned to the source of the voice. The old man looked up at her.

"Lydia Carver," he said.

"No, my name is Rachel." She smiled and moved away through the crowd.

"Must be gettin' old." She heard the voice faintly as it was swallowed up by the loudspeaker announcing the three-legged race. "Lydia Carver had green eyes."

THE FOUR-PIECE BAND from Loyalton was playing an old swing standard when Rachel arrived at the dance. She had gone back to Gran's for dinner and to change into her dusky rose dress with the camisole top. It was one of her favorites. She loved the lace and ribbon insert in a more golden shade that threaded across her breasts and wove in and out of the calf-length, gathered skirt. She had swept her hair up in a Gibson style to complement the romantic mood of the dress. Her high-heeled sandals, the pinkish color of Black Hills gold, and the beaded Victorian bag completed the outfit. The fringed antique piano shawl would be enough protection from the gentle evening breezes.

It was a look Rachel rarely indulged in, hinting as it did of times long past when women were cosseted and protected by their men. She herself was nothing if not a contemporary woman, leading an independent life, running a business of her own. But still she had a right occasionally to feel one hundred percent feminine. This particular dress always ensured that she would.

The upstairs dance floor of the community hall was already full of swirling couples. She picked out Gran and Gideon doing their best in the center of the floor—Gran always did have a tendency to lead.

Gideon flashed Rachel his lopsided grin. Gran waved.

"How's the weather up there, beautiful?"

Rachel whirled at the sound of a familiar voice.

"Tommy Seevers." Her lips curved in a welcoming smile.

"God, Rachel. You look terrific. Should have swept you off your feet back at the senior prom when I had the chance."

"Well, it's a little too late now." Her throaty laugh brought an answering grin from Tommy. Rachel shared many happy memories with the dark-haired, handsome man who stood beside her.

"Yeah, Alaina's got me roped, tied and branded, all right. But she's too busy takin' tickets to dance. How 'bout you?"

"I thought you'd never ask." She went into the friendly circle of his arms. Their bodies moved together with a comfortable precision. Tommy was an excellent dancer, and Rachel had been his partner more than once. They dipped and swayed effortlessly through the maze of moving couples.

The band had struck up an energetic polka when she caught sight of Kane. He was standing near the double doors that led out to the long balcony. His toast-brown slacks and raw silk jacket contrasted with the jeans and Western shirts of most of the men around him, but somehow he didn't look in the least out of place. He had even dared to wear a tie, which a willowy redhead was straightening solicitously.

"That was my foot, beautiful," Tommy said as they swung around again and bounced past the bandstand.

"Sorry." Rachel didn't like the breathless sound of her laugh. "I thought you had a spare."

Billy Short asked her to dance next. A stockily built amateur mechanic, Billy had broken his mother's heart when he'd dropped out of school after the eighth grade. He had the kind of grease under his fingernails that just wouldn't wash off and an irritating way of treating all women as if they were cuddly little stuffed toys with sawdust between their ears. In the interests of chivalry, before requesting a dance he had put aside the stub of a cold cigar that he usually held clamped between his teeth. His head came exactly to Rachel's breasts, and she had to stifle a naughty chuckle more than once when he tried to carry on a conversation with her, addressing instead the ripe mounds at eye level.

Kane waltzed by, the redhead in his arms. The woman was laughing up at him, a dreamy, half-teasing expression on her face. Rachel's involuntary sigh was wistful. The two did make a lovely couple.

Rachel had danced with Chris and Gideon and a host of old friends and near relatives by the time she went out on the balcony to gaze up at the stars. The evening air had grown chilly, so she gathered the shawl close around her shoulders.

Leaning out on the railing, she watched the moths beat at the lamps across the street above the Miners' Museum, thinking that the sturdy, slate-walled building was filled with treasures, both from the mines and from the people who had worked them. Oh, there was no place on earth like this mountain community in which she had grown to womanhood. There was an aura here, distinctly American, an almost speaking promise in the air. It said that with a pick and shovel and a bit of blessed luck, a man might make his dreams reality.

Rachel closed her eyes and drank in the moment. It was so near to perfection. It needed only one element to make it complete.

A gentle hand grazed her cheekbone, smoothing a wandering strand of hair behind the pink shell of her ear.

"Dance with me."

The dark fringe of her lashes swept up. Gold-flecked eyes met smoky quartz. Something coiled warm in her belly. It was the night and the speaking promise in the air. It was the soft strains that drifted from the hall beyond. It was this man, who had materialized as if at the command of her idle, half-formed fantasy.

Her hand came up of its own free will. Her fingers fluttered like moth wings against the sandpaper cheek. With infinite, slow gentleness, his mouth reached to brush her lips. The kiss was feather soft, a tender salute to a passion not vanquished, but stilled now for this one moment of suspended time. His nostrils flared slightly, and his sharp intake of breath told her more than she wanted to know.

"No one smells like you." The resonant tones were almost a whisper. The heat of his nearness had released her scent; it mingled with the dusky essence of Caleche, her signature perfume. The coiled warmth in her belly went liquid. He took her hand and led her back inside.

It was a slow number. Kane's arms were satin over steel around her, but he was careful not to press her too close. He seemed content, for now, to move with her to the rhythm of the dance, letting their bodies brush tender, a subtle seduction.

When the dance ended, they stood near the edge of the floor. His arms fell away. She had to catch herself from swaying back against him. He smiled at her, his expression quizzical.

"What you are, Rachel, is too many women for one man to keep track of."

She didn't answer. She only needed to still the beating of her heart and then she could walk away. Gran came up to them, Gideon in tow.

"It's our generous Mr. Walker," Gran announced. "You've met Kane Walker, Gideon?"

"Yep," Gideon replied, never a one to waste words.

"Having a nice time, dear?" Gran made no effort to conceal the twinkle in her dark eyes. She turned back to Kane. "Chris just told me you've invited us all up to your place for a barbecue Saturday. I think that would be delightful. Don't you, Rachel?"

"I . . . uh—"

"Good. I'm sure we'll have a wonderful time. I have so looked forward to a tour of your new house, Mr. Walker."

"Call me Kane. We are neighbors after all, Mrs. Carver." The two grinned at each other like conspirators. "Would you like to dance?"

"Only if you'll address me as Ethel." Gran stepped primly into Kane's arms. They waltzed off together.

"A force of nature, your grandmother." Gideon's parched cackle sounded beside her. "Well, don't just stand there, gal. I got me a yen to dance with someone who knows how to follow."

Gideon stretched out his gnarled hand. Rachel took it, realized her mouth was hanging open and snapped it firmly shut.

3

RACHEL LOOKED UP from the Scrabble board and glared at her grandmother. "I'm not buying that."

"You'll have to challenge me, then." Gran's angelic smile spoke volumes; she was winning and quite pleased with herself.

"Honestly, Gran. If you're going to invent words, you could at least make them believable." Rachel shoved the sleeves of her bulky cable-knit pullover farther up her arms. "There is no such thing as a 'quaich.'"

"Ah, but there is."

"Define it."

"Now, dear, you know I don't have to do that." Gran patted the huge old dictionary on the stand beside her. "Shall we look it up?"

Rachel chewed on her scoring pencil, considering. She had already challenged Gran twice this game, and lost two turns in the bargain. She shifted in her chair, bringing one foot up under her.

"If I lose another turn I'll probably lose the game." With the pencil between her teeth, Rachel readjusted one of the combs that held back her hair.

"Don't squirm, dear. It doesn't suit you."

"I'm not squirming, I'm thinking." Taking the pencil in her fingers again, Rachel tapped it on the table and glanced out the window.

All thoughts of the game fled at the sight of Chris's pickup turning into the lot by the schoolhouse and backing into her grandmother's driveway. Her cousin wasn't alone; Kane was with him. Nat ran out to meet them.

Hardly aware of her own action, Rachel stuck the pencil in her mouth again. She bit down; the soft wood gave way with a satisfying crunch.

"My goodness," said Gran, "I'd forgotten."

"What?" Rachel tossed the mangled pencil aside.

"Lydia's things. Chris told me he'd be down tonight to take them to the dump."

There was a tap on the door. Rachel twisted in her chair as her cousin came inside. Kane was right behind.

Despising herself for the quickening of her heartbeat, Rachel drank in the sight of him. Besides the inevitable khaki pants and lace-up boots, he had on an old flannel shirt rolled to the elbows. Soft from many washings, the worn fabric hinted at the broad expanse of chest beneath.

"Sarah sent me out to pick up a carton of milk before I headed down here—and guess who I ran into?" Chris clapped a hand on Kane's shoulder.

"So of course you decided to put him to work." Laying her pencil on top of her scoresheet, Gran rose to her feet.

Chris pretended to look guilty. "I tried not to take advantage of him, but he said he didn't mind."

"I figured I might as well make myself useful." Kane's tone was unassuming, offhand. The faint, parenthetical grooves at the sides of his mouth deepened in an easy smile.

I'll bet, Rachel thought, gripping the back of her chair. First he'd followed her to the Cliffs. Then he had just happened to be every place she'd gone yesterday. And now he'd manipulated her cousin into bringing him here.

Say something, her mind ordered angrily. *Show him that he has absolutely no effect on you!*

"We could have managed by ourselves." It came out all wrong. Snappish. Rude.

Gran's lips pursed. Chris's bushy brows drew together.

Mentally Rachel counted to three and tried again. "Don't mind me." She waved a hand at the Scrabble board. "I'm losing." She felt the tension around her relax.

Chris let out a short laugh. "You should be used to it by now, String Bean. Grandma always wins—one way or another."

Gran sighed exaggeratedly. "My grandchildren have always maintained that I cheat."

"Do you?" Kane asked, joining in the family banter as if he were a part of it.

"Only when necessary." Gran was already in the short hallway that led to the stairs. "Come along, Christopher. I'll show you what needs to be done."

With an easygoing shrug, Chris did as his grandmother ordered. Rachel waited for Kane to follow after them, but he showed no inclination to leave his spot by the door. The soft, worn material of his shirt gave then clung like a gentle lover with each breath he took.

Rachel turned and faced the table. Picking up the chewed pencil once more, she concentrated on the marks of her own teeth embedded in the soft wood. She could feel his dark eyes on her back.

His hand reached over her shoulder and lifted the pencil from her grasp. "What did this pencil ever do to you?" The rough, deep voice was in her ear, the sharp, woodsy scent of him teasing her nostrils. She wondered distractedly if he could hear the rapid pounding of her heart.

Mercifully he moved away, coming around the table and into her line of vision. The overhead light cast a gilding brightness over his brows and hair.

Rachel stood up. "I thought you came to help out."

"I did." He was grinning.

"The job starts upstairs."

He stuck her pencil behind an ear. "I realize that."

Above them she could hear Gran giving instructions, Chris grunting amiably in agreement. Kane crossed his arms over his chest and went on grinning.

"Well, what are you waiting for?" Rachel said through clenched teeth.

"You." He took the pencil in his fingers again. "If I give this back, do you promise not to eat it?"

With a supreme effort of will Rachel suppressed the invectives that rose to her lips. Light. She had resolved to keep things light. If she lost her temper now she would be giving him just what he wanted.

Changing tactics abruptly, she held out her hand. "All right." He returned the pencil. "Thank you."

"You're welcome."

Her smile was etched in acid. "Follow me."

"Glad to." He was close behind her as she mounted the first step.

Chris flattened himself against the opposite wall when they reached the top, a box of old bottles clinking and shifting in his arms. The space at the head of the stairs was too small for all of them, so Kane moved to one of the dormer windows that looked out over the street.

Gran was on her knees, riffling through a stack of tattered catalogs. "I'm sure it was here somewhere."

"What, Gran?" Rachel slid out of the way as Chris edged around her and down the stairs.

"The wedding photo. I thought I set it on the bed table in the other room, but now it's gone. You didn't happen to . . . pick it up?"

Gran was looking at her apprehensively. Rachel reminded herself that there was no reason to feel guilty. Her urge to burn the snapshot had not been carried out. Still she felt somehow culpable—as if the desire to destroy had actually been translated into action.

Rachel was painfully aware of Kane's waiting calmly by the window, of eyes that missed nothing, of sharp ears that would be alert for any evidence of weakness to use against her. And her unresolved feelings about her parents were definitely a weakness, one she had always contrived to keep from him at the time when he'd ruled her heart.

"It's the only picture I have of the two of them," Gran prodded gently.

"I know that." Rachel's voice was strained as she forced it through the constriction in her throat. "I put it inside the front cover of one of the albums downstairs—the maroon one with the shoestring bindings."

The worried tightness in Gran's face eased. Leaning heavily on the stack of catalogs, she brought herself upright. "Good. I would have hated to have lost it."

Rachel pointed to the boxes along a far wall, anxious to reassure her grandmother that she had done a thorough inventory of Lydia's things. "Everything that could possibly be of use to anyone is in those boxes, ready for the next rummage sale. I left the nicer bottles, her school things and all her favorite books in my room, if you want to check through them again."

Gran shook her head. "No. Let it go." She seemed to be talking to herself as much as to Rachel. "I'm sure you made all the right choices."

Gran turned to Kane, smiling wryly. "I've spent my life taking charge, but something tells me right now I should stay out of the way."

"Not always the easiest thing to do," Kane remarked, managing to sound sympathetic and politely detached at the same time.

Chris was coming back up the stairs. Gran waited for him to reach the top before descending herself. Hefting a stack of catalogs, Chris headed down behind her.

Kane came away from the window. "Not that much here," he said casually, kneeling, piling two stacks of catalog wishbooks on top of a box. "This stuff was your mother's?"

"Yes. Gran had stored all her things in the closet in my room. But now with Gideon . . . Gran needs the space." Rachel caught her lower lip in her teeth. The simple explanation had come out charged with emotions she didn't want to acknowledge.

An elusive light flared in Kane's eyes and was gone. "You never told me much about your parents." He was levering the box against his chest now, rising easily to stand beside her.

She avoided his gaze, focusing instead on his forearms wrapped around the rough cardboard of the box, on the ridges of tendon beneath bronze skin.

"They died when I was so young, I hardly remember them." She kept her voice carefully level but still found it impossible to meet his eyes.

Down below, Chris's heavy tread could be heard approaching the stairs again. Rachel bent swiftly and scooped up the last of the catalogs. Without looking back, she started down the steps.

"Come on," she called over her shoulder. "I thought you were here to help out."

"I am, Rachel. I am" came the quiet reply.

Chris invited her along when they were through loading up. Rachel made her excuses. After all, there was the Scrabble game to finish.

"See you Saturday," Kane reminded them as he swung into the truck on the passenger side. "Around six?"

"Six o'clock," Gran confirmed with alacrity. The truck pulled away from them and into the street. Gran turned to Rachel. "I believe that young man is still fond of you."

Rachel forced a tight smile. "You're mistaken. He likes you, and he gets along well with Chris. That's all. There's been nothing between Kane and me for years."

"I never understood why you stopped seeing him. That summer you brought him here for a visit, you seemed to get on so well together."

"We were kids, Gran. We grew out of each other." The words had a flat finality, just as she'd intended.

"I see." Gran tugged the cardigan she had thrown across her shoulders closer. "It's cool this evening. Shall we go back inside?"

All around were the sounds of mountain night—the lazy croaking of frogs by the ditch across the road, the songs of the crickets, the low-pitched roar of the river under all. Rachel barely heard them.

Saturday—the day after tomorrow—her family expected her to spend a whole evening under the gaze of those brown-black eyes. It was too much to ask. But getting out of it would mean confessing the mess her emotions were in—or fabricating some reason why she just couldn't go. Neither alternative held much appeal.

"Rachel?"

"Um? Oh. Yes. Cool. We should go inside."

The Scrabble game ended predictably. Rachel lost by two hundred points. As they loaded the tiles and board away in the box, Rachel seriously considered the idea of confiding in Gran. But what would she say? That the nice young man who had invited them to dinner had the morals of an alley cat? That he seduced married women to get financing for his health-club empire? That he had built his cabin up Goodyears Creek Road with the express purpose of tormenting Rachel to distraction?

It sounded so . . . tawdry. Gran would be shocked.

And how much could she tell? If she were to be completely honest, she would have to admit that her pain at Kane's betrayal had been tinged with something very close to relief.

Her feelings for Kane had always been hard to handle. From the first she'd been afraid of an attraction so overwhelming it threatened to upset her well-ordered existence. A part of her had been grateful when it was finally finished between them. And knowing Rachel's strong need for independence, Gran would wonder if Kane's unpardonable behavior had merely hastened the inevitable.

Then, too, Gran and Kane seemed to get along so well. Gran would be bewildered and hurt to think she had so misjudged another human being. And ultimately what could Gran be expected to do? Throw his dinner invitation in his face? Have Gideon challenge him to a duel? Call up everyone in town and tell them to watch out for Kane Walker?

No, Gran would listen, sympathize—and worry. And her concern would cast a shadow over her pleasure in her coming marriage to Gideon.

RACHEL WAS IN BED with a book propped up against her knees to distract her from the tangle of her thoughts. The phone rang downstairs.

"Rachel? Dear? It's for you!"

"Coming!" Marking her place and laying the book on the nightstand, Rachel pulled on her robe and went down to answer.

"It's Los Angeles. Mrs. Springer. I think she said something about . . . coffee cups?" Gran handed Rachel the phone and disappeared into the bathroom.

"Yes, Elaine. What is it?"

"You could say hello. Don't I rate hello?" the voice in her ear teased with a scratchy, deep-throated chuckle.

Her assistant's laughter almost made Rachel wish she were back in L.A. hard at work, so busy that thoughts of Kane Walker would have to be stamped "low priority" and filed at the back of a very deep bottom drawer.

Rachel sighed. "Hello, Elaine."

"That's better." Elaine let out a mollified snort.

"Have you got a problem?" Rachel asked hopefully.

Elaine was very efficient. She had once told Rachel there was no such thing as a problem—only challenges to be triumphantly overcome.

"Problem? No problem. A couple of minor challenges to be met, that's all. Since you're the boss, I thought I'd get a few suggestions from you before deciding what to do."

"I really appreciate that," Rachel said dryly.

"I knew you would," Elaine replied with another snort. "The first concerns the WLG Cable benefit. . . ."

Rachel shifted the phone to her other ear. The benefit was a big one, set for the following evening. Fifteen hundred guests and a Moulin Rouge theme. She and Elaine had gone over all the plans in mind-bending detail before Rachel's departure; there shouldn't have been any unforeseen glitches. But, of course, there always were.

"It's the rentals," Elaine explained. "You know the gold-leaf china pattern? Well, the rental company shorted us a thousand on the coffee cups. I only discovered it this afternoon when I did the equipment tally."

"You called them?"

"Of course. They said how sorry they were, but our cups had been rerented by accident and they would give us a huge future credit to make up for the error, as well as any other china they had on hand free of charge for tomorrow night—"

"And none of it will do, and you've called all over town and no one has anything resembling what you need," Rachel finished, her lips curving in a knowing smile.

"Exactly. Your suggestion?"

"Call the original rental company back," Rachel began with crisp authority. "Tell them you want fifteen hundred extra wineglasses in place of the cups."

"Wineglasses? Rachel, I've got wineglasses. What good is fifteen hundred extra going to do me?"

"Will you let me finish?" Rachel inquired in silky tones, grinning at Gran, who was emerging from the bathroom.

"Well. All right."

With Elaine effectively quelled, Rachel continued. "Just standard wineglasses, the simpler the better. Then tomorrow night, when it's time for the coffee and dessert crepes, you give them . . . Café parisien!"

"What's that?"

"Cinnamon and sugar, half coffee, half whipped cream. Oh, and a lemon wedge. Stick a maraschino cherry on top. It's served in a wineglass. They'll love it."

"Rachel, you're a genius."

"No, just resourceful. What else?"

Elaine lowered her voice. "Is your grandmother still in the room? Have you told her what you're doing for the wedding?"

"Yes. And no."

"Okay. I get it. She's still in the room. You haven't told her. It's still a surprise."

"That's it," Rachel answered cautiously, shooting a sidelong glance at Gran, who had perched herself on the couch. "Now what about it?"

"Well, Max and Kelly are all yours. They'll be there the day before with the truck."

"What about Ralf?"

Rachel needed Ralf for his ability with floral arrangements. Neither Max nor Carlos was much good in that particular area.

"The flowers, I know," Elaine said ruefully. "But I got a call from Nancy Taylor. She's having a small dinner party that same evening. She specifically requested Ralf."

"How about Kelly?"

"For Mrs. Taylor?" Elaine sniffed with disdain. "It's French service, Rachel. Mrs. Taylor doesn't want personality. She wants smooth efficiency and an eye for detail. She wants Ralf's best imitation of butler to the crowned heads of Europe."

"No. I didn't mean Kelly for Mrs. Taylor," Rachel said, careful of her phrasing. "I mean . . . Kelly's quite good with flowers, right?"

"Oh! For the wedding? *You'll* take Kelly?"

"Why not? It's casual, you understand? Kelly will be fine."

"All right. I'll ask her."

"Great. Is that all?"

Elaine let out her scratchy laugh. "That's all. Go to bed, Rachel."

"Good night, Elaine." Rachel hung up the phone.

Gran was feeling around in the pockets of her quilted pink robe. "Total disaster averted once again?" Producing her bifocals, she set them on the end of her nose and peered up at Rachel in wry amusement. "Café parisien? I don't believe I've ever tried it."

"Probably because I just made it up." Rachel plopped down on the couch beside her grandmother, relieved that the older woman had sensed nothing suspicious in her last oblique exchange with Elaine.

The idea of keeping the wedding theme a surprise seemed more and more the right approach. Gran was so used to being in control. It would save a lot of wear and tear on everyone if she didn't know until it was too late to change things that Rachel had planned otherwise. Of course, it really wasn't playing fair, but Rachel soothed a nagging conscience by telling herself that the subterfuge was motivated by love.

Gran wrapped an arm around Rachel's shoulder. "Not only resourceful but imaginative, too. You must have been brought up in a creative environment."

"I was." Rachel laid her cheek on pink-quilted softness, sighing contentedly as she caught the faint scents of mint mouthwash and lavender eau de toilette . . . good smells. To Rachel they meant all that was warm and loving and wise in the world.

The thought of sharing her worries about Kane crept into her mind again. But where to begin . . .

No, she chided herself silently, it wasn't Gran's problem. She would keep her own counsel, as she always had. Whatever Kane Walker's game, she would best him at it alone.

4

A FINE DEW of sweat moistened her brow as Rachel reached the top of the steep cut. Taking a moment to catch her breath, she watched a blue-belly lizard shoot across the road and up the serpentine bank to her right. Nat made a little noise in his throat but stayed at her heels.

The rest of her walk was downhill, along the road that was no longer the highway, then into a small glen where the trees made the late-morning air much cooler. She collected Gran's mail and was out on the post office steps reading the movie poster of coming attractions in Downieville when the Land Rover pulled in.

With that sinewy, lithe grace she knew so well, Kane jumped to the ground and mounted the steps toward her. He hadn't bothered to put on a shirt, and she was forced to confront the bronze chest and the V of springy gold hairs across and down it.

Nat sniffed at his lace-up boots. Kane knelt and scratched the dog under the chin. The baggy khakis stretched more tautly across his thighs.

"Sometimes I think you're following me around." His voice held that infuriating, teasing note. He looked up from under a shock of tawny hair.

"I . . . I'm following you?"

"Nice dog."

"He belongs to Gran."

"I know."

"Well, anyway. . . I'm glad I ran into you because—"

"You are?" He came to his feet again and grinned down at her. "I'm glad you're glad." The man was impossible.

"I wanted to tell you . . . that I won't be able to make it for dinner tomorrow. I—there's so much to do, with the wedding and all . . ."

"You look cute in cutoffs." He was still smiling, but the tensing had begun at his jaw.

"I'm trying to tell you . . ." She could see the post office clerk through the screen door. He had looked up from sorting the mail.

"Planning on having a headache? Going to lie down with a wet rag over your eyes and tell your grandmother you don't feel up to a barbecue at Kane Walker's?"

"Of course not." The clerk was definitely staring now.

"Good. Then I'll see you tomorrow evening. Now if you'll excuse me, I want to get my mail." The screen door banged shut behind him as he went inside.

Nat wagged his tail and bumped the hand Rachel had clenched at her side. She felt like banging more than a screen door. Wasn't he ever going to realize that she wanted nothing to do with him or his barbecues or his neighborly offers to haul junk to the dump?

The sight of the spying postal clerk, as he made a valiant effort to drag his gaze back to the stack of envelopes in his hand, stopped her. Rachel took off down the short steps at a run.

"C'mon, Nat! Race you to the highway!"

The dog allowed her a moment's lead, then shot off the porch, passing her easily, stopping several yards ahead to give a gleeful bark of encouragement. Rachel indulged in a nice full-out run down the cut, slowing at the bridge to walk the rest of the way. By the time she reached

Gran's, she was sweating heavily and feeling much calmer.

Gran was out in the garden. Rachel took the mail into the house, then went to help pick green beans for dinner.

It was Gran who spotted the frost-white Seville first. "Why, dear, I believe we have company."

The car rounded the corner from the bridge and floated toward them, white sidewalls pristine in the afternoon sun. The woman behind the wheel waved at them and drove past to pull into the schoolyard across from the house.

Rachel tossed a fistful of beans into an almost-full bucket. Straightening, she caught her lower lip between her teeth and chewed for a moment at the inner flesh of her mouth. It was an old nervous habit, one she thought she'd broken long ago. "Catherine," she said. "What's she doing here?"

"I suppose she's come for the wedding." Gran appeared as taken aback as Rachel felt.

"You invited her?"

"It seemed only polite. But I didn't really expect her to come. And over a week early, too...."

A little dismayed, Rachel looked down at her ragged cutoffs and sweat-stained tank top. She had always been careful to look her best around Catherine; it made her feel more the proud old woman's equal. She stole a glance at Gran, who had tugged the wide straw hat from her head and was tucking stray hairs back into her French braids.

"Well," said Gran, handing Rachel the bucket, "standing here gawking is certainly no way to welcome a guest."

Clutching the pail, Rachel followed Gran up through the garden and around the side path that led to the front gate.

"You're looking well, Rachel Diane." The cheek like fine pink parchment was held up for Rachel to kiss. "It's lovely to see you, Ethel." The wrinkled rosebud mouth smiled at Gran.

"This *is* a surprise," Gran replied. "We . . . weren't expecting you quite so soon."

A perfectly manicured hand strayed up to the ruffle that concealed the age lines at Catherine's neck. "I know I should have called." The words came out in an uncharacteristic rush. "But I didn't know myself until . . . I rarely do anything on impulse as you know, but since I got your invitation I haven't been able to think of anything else. That old house of mine seemed so . . . lonely somehow. And I knew Rachel would be here. . . ." The flood of explanations broke off. Rachel realized that Catherine was the one on unfamiliar ground. "I'm sure I can get a room in Downieville, don't you think? I only just stopped by to—"

"Nonsense," Gran interrupted, suddenly firm. "You'll stay here with us."

"It was truly not my intention to impose." Opal-gray eyes were focused on Rachel.

Rachel kept her expression carefully blank. It was never Catherine's intention to impose; she just did it. Naturally.

"You can have the other room upstairs," Rachel said. "We all have to share the bathtub," she added, thinking of Catherine's big old house in San Francisco where every bedroom had an adjoining bath.

"I don't mind. Not at all." Catherine sounded honestly grateful.

Rachel reminded herself that Catherine had always given the impression of an exquisite, fragile piece of fine china, that the steely will beneath the delicate veneer was never immediately apparent. Still there did seem to be a new vulnerability about her today.

"I'm sure you'd like to freshen up after your drive." Gran put an arm around Catherine's shoulders and took the bucket of green beans from Rachel's hand. "Rachel will bring your things inside."

"EVERYTHING IS SO VERY...FRESH," Catherine said enthusiastically.

Rachel speared a piece of flank steak and brought it to her mouth.

"Both food value and flavor are so much higher when one grows one's own," Gran intoned.

Rachel kept her eyes studiously on her plate. Her grandmothers had been exchanging excruciating pleasantries for five and one-quarter hours, not including Catherine's brief nap between two and three.

"Oh, Ethel. You're absolutely correct," Catherine agreed, daintily raising a section of green bean to her rosebud mouth. She chewed it thoroughly and then turned to Rachel.

"What imaginative design have you concocted for the wedding, Rachel Diane?"

"Gran wants it simple. Paper plates and pot luck, I think. A sort of community picnic with everybody pitching in."

"But surely, Ethel, you'll at least allow Rachel to—"

"It's Gran's wedding," Rachel said.

"Well. Certainly." Catherine busied herself with her salad.

"Shall we take our coffee out on the porch?" Gran suggested brightly.

"You two go ahead. I'll just clean up these dishes first." Rachel picked up her plate and carried it to the sink. "I was thinking afterward I might go for a walk."

Rachel felt a little guilty deserting Gran. But she had to have a moment to herself now and then.

Surprisingly, Gran didn't object. "Take Nat," she said. "He always enjoys a good walk."

When the dishes were done Rachel took her light jacket and headed up the Old Road toward the swinging bridge. Dusk was an hour or so away, but the evening coolness was already coming on. The sun itself had gone beneath the hills.

The unpaved ground crunched under her shoes, and the roar of the river tumbling just beyond the trees to her left was a comforting sound. She stopped at the power house and made her way to the rocky bank.

Nat stood beside her on the little promontory where she used to fish so often, years ago. They watched the swallows dive for insects, swooping down from nowhere, skimming the surface and rising, smooth as kites, back to the sky. On top of the sheer cliff across the river, cars went rushing past, bound for Downieville or Grass Valley.

This vacation wasn't shaping up as she had planned at all. Kane, who was easy enough to avoid in L.A., seemed to turn up everywhere in this small community. He was filling her dreams again with his brown-black eyes and wood-smoke laugh. And he was worming his way into the affections of her family, too, until they almost behaved as if he belonged here.

And now Catherine had arrived. Ten days with Catherine. It was a lot to ask. Ten days of the opal-gray eyes, the same hauntingly pale color as her father's had been.

Rachel never thought of her father except when she looked at Catherine. It was almost bearable in San Francisco. But here, so close to the spirit of Lydia, it became a war inside her. The legacy of pain inherited from her parents could not overwhelm her as long as she kept them separate in her mind. And most of the time, she managed to do just that—the same way she kept the various components of her life comfortably separate. She had her career in L.A., made obligatory yearly visits to Catherine in San Francisco and found the mountains of the Sierra foothills a place where she could relax and be herself. That was why Kane, and Catherine, too, threatened her balance, made her fear some kind of dangerous merging of one world into the other.

Rachel sat down and gathered her legs up under her chin, leaning her head on them, willing the sense of vague apprehension, her constant companion lately, to leave her in peace. Nat gave an airy snort and flopped down beside her.

To her right, a depression in the hard rock made a channel that emptied into a small pool of about a foot in diameter. The water in the pool—a puddle, really—was a few inches deep. Rachel leaned back on an elbow and watched the minnows that had found their way there swimming perkily around. Poor minnows. How could they know that as the waterline receded, the channel would dry up, leaving them stranded.

A sluggish movement caught her eye. Even in the waning light, she picked out the inch-long stick that crawled along the bottom.

"It's a periwinkle, Rachel. They live in creek shallows and tug their log-shaped houses around behind them. Just like a snail with his shell. . . ." She could hear Lydia's voice in her mind as if Lydia were with her now.

Rachel sat upright and hugged her knees again. She smiled.

Memories of her parents were usually dangerous, leading to painful scenes of confrontation and, ultimately, loss. But there had been that one summer when Rachel was eight, the summer Lydia and Rachel had come together to visit Gran. For those few short months Rachel had seen a side of Lydia that surprised and delighted her. The pale, withdrawn stranger Rachel had learned to call mother became another person entirely—a magic person who wore her torn, ill-fitting jeans with easy grace, who smiled often and rose even before Gran to make breakfast for the three of them.

Together Rachel and Lydia had scoured old mine sites for buried bottles, picked baskets full of blackberries for jam, gone swimming nearly every day at Lydia's favorite spot, the Cliffs.

It was the end of summer when Rachel's father had finally come himself to bring them back. Lydia had at first refused to go. But in the end, as always, Catherine's son got his way. They had returned to San Francisco, where the vibrant, earthy side of Lydia disappeared, never to be glimpsed again.

Rachel shivered and came to her feet, stuffing her hands into the pockets of her jacket.

"Let's go, Nat," she said, turning away from the river and back to the road.

A pink and purple blush colored the hills to the west by the time Rachel returned to Gran's. She could hear the soft babble of voices from the side porch. Nat went to his water bowl as Rachel crossed through the yard to the stairs that accessed the porch from the front. Both of her grandmothers were sitting in lounge chairs, facing off toward the vegetable garden.

"I see now why Phillip fell in love with this place," Catherine was saying softly.

Rachel hesitated on the second step, tensing at the mention of her father's name.

"I often think he would have been glad to spend more time up here if I hadn't been so . . . if I had been more supportive of him. And of Lydia."

"Now, Catherine. You mustn't blame yourself. They were from different worlds. It was very difficult for either of them to adjust to the changes their marriage demanded. Lydia was always more than I could understand. I used to worry about her so. She had none of the interests of other young girls. I confess I never thought she would marry at all."

"Is there any coffee left?" Rachel asked, making her presence known.

The tiny, sharp intake of Catherine's breath told Rachel that her grandmother wondered how much she had overheard. Rachel studied the fine old face in the waning light. There *was* a change in Catherine. What was it? A softening, perhaps from all the years alone in that big house since the death of her son? The opal-gray eyes had lost that contradictory intolerance, were shadowed now with a sadness and a need . . . for what? Forgiveness?

"Gran is right," Rachel said, suddenly feeling an alarming urge to get it all out in the open. "There's no sense in blaming yourself. The two of them never should have married in the first place. And if it hadn't been for me, they wouldn't have." Gran cleared her throat. Catherine was fiddling with her collar. "And as for my father, he was too busy making sure Hays, Gardner and Davis stayed the top legal firm in the state to have much time for vacations in the hills." The flat sound of her own voice startled even Rachel. It seemed the words had come of their own accord, that someone else was saying these things.

"Your father loved you very much," Catherine was saying.

Rachel took her lower lip between her teeth, caught herself succumbing to the childish habit and released it. Both of her grandmothers were looking at her with a curious mixture of regret and pity.

"Please don't look at me like that. And don't try to explain it away. It's the truth, and it's better if we face it like it is."

"What exactly do you mean when you say 'the truth,' dear?" Gran asked gently. They were ganging up on her, these two women with nothing in common.

"Lydia wasn't meant to get married. You said it yourself, Gran. She would have been happy with her Sears and Roebuck wishbooks, combing the hills for old bottles, off in her own world somewhere in baggy pants and beat-up boots . . . with the river and trees for company. And Phillip should have married a Nob Hill socialite like Catherine wanted him to!"

"They were very much in love," Catherine said.

"Love!" Rachel spat the word. "He wanted her and he got her pregnant and he married her. He always knew what he wanted, and he always made sure he got it—even if he didn't know what to do with it afterward!"

Catherine half rose from her chair. Her arms reached out. The gesture was pleading—involuntary. Not like the Catherine Rachel knew at all.

Rachel shrank back. "No . . . no, don't touch me . . ." she heard her own voice say weakly.

She was shocked at herself, at the things she'd just said out loud about her father. Never in her life had she let her secret feelings come clawing to the surface like that. What was happening to her?

As quickly as she formed the question, the answer came: Kane. He had succeeded in pushing her close to the emotional edge by putting himself in her path so often these past few days. And now she was forced to deal with Catherine—this strange, gentle Catherine who begged for tolerance and understanding.

Worse, Rachel's churning emotions were stirring up memories. Like the rolling smoke from a forest fire, the past was all around her, swirling, clutching, cutting off her breath.

As if it were happening that moment, she saw her parents kissing in the foyer of Catherine's San Francisco house, so absorbed in the heat between them that they were unaware of the child who watched them from the stairwell. "God, Liddy. I'll never have enough of you...." Phillip had groaned.

Then, superimposed over the image of her parents, she witnessed herself and Kane, locked in a similar embrace in the kitchen of her apartment in L.A. "Lord, Rachel. It's like I'll never get enough of you...."

Willing the images to disappear, Rachel forced her lungs to expand. For brief seconds she was back on the porch. Catherine was standing in front of her, hands hanging limply at her sides.

But the past was not through with Rachel yet. The very air she drew in sent her spinning back in time. The air was clean. Sharp with the scent of pine. Pine. Kane always smelled of pine.

"Don't touch me." She had said it to Catherine just now. It was the same thing she had said to Kane six years before, on the night of the party when Mariette Sayer had announced she was financing the creation of a new concept in health clubs. A concept based on the expertise and personal philosophy of Kane Walker.

After the announcement, Rachel had only wanted to get away. But Kane had caught her at the dessert table, grabbing her arm before she could flee again.

"I wanted to tell you before we made it public, but you've been avoiding me for days."

"Don't touch me, Kane." She tried to jerk free. He gripped her arm more tightly. "If you must manhandle someone," she whispered silkily, "try Mariette. I imagine she likes it."

"Mariette's been good to both of us," he reminded her with icy tightness. "She's a true friend to me. And now she's decided to put her money behind me because she knows it's a good investment. That's all."

"Mariette." The name came out like a curse. "You can tell your precious Mariette that this is the last party I'll design for her. I don't work for married women who indulge in tacky affairs with their aerobics instructors."

The brown-threaded black eyes went hard as agates, while the sensual lips drew back in a cruel sneer. "Why don't you admit Mariette's got nothing to do with this?" He yanked her closer. His breath was hot on her face. "It was fine between us as long as I was just a pizza slinger teaching aerobics on the side. I was safe then, wasn't I, Rachel? But you can't stand the idea of loving a man who knows what he wants from life. Then you wouldn't have control, would you?"

A few of the people near them had turned to stare. Kane saw the pain on her face, mingled with her embarrassment. He released her. "Sorry. I know how you hate a scene."

He spun away from her then and stalked off. She rubbed absently at the red marks his fingers had made on her flesh. A waiter passed by, balancing a tray laden with bubbling champagne. She reached for one of the fluted glasses. When she brought it to her lips, it spilled, staining the sleek satin of her gown.

"Rachel? Rachel Diane?"

Rachel shook her head. The haze of memory receded, and Catherine's stricken face swam into focus once more. Rachel gritted her teeth, ordering her mind to stay in the now. But the clutching fingers of the past still had hold of her, dragging her back, farther back than before.

"Don't touch me…." Lydia had said that to Phillip the night they'd both died. The night of the accident.

Rachel saw herself clearly as she had been that night, a ten-year-old girl in a frilly lace dress. It was a drizzly May evening. Her parents had taken her to the zoo, then to dinner at Fisherman's Wharf. It was supposed to have been a special time, a whole day just for her, because it was her birthday. But the day had gone as sour as the weather.

It had started at the zoo. Lydia had become more withdrawn than usual as they moved from cage to cage, her lovely face a mask that hid her thoughts. And at the restaurant on the wharf, she wouldn't talk to her husband or her child. She glared down at the lobster Phillip had ordered for her, shook her head mutely when asked if she'd have dessert.

On the way home, Phillip, bewildered as always by the brooding cipher his wife could become, tried to smooth things over.

"Come on, Liddy. It's Rachel's birthday." He took one hand from the wheel and tried to draw Lydia closer to him.

"Don't touch me." Lydia huddled against the passenger door.

In the back seat Rachel watched them, chewing her lip, clutching the box of chocolate éclairs Phillip had bought her before they got in the car. Éclairs were Rachel's favorite dessert. Phillip had promised her a whole one to herself before she went to bed.

"You can't keep me here. I want to go home!" Lydia demanded on a rising inflection.

Phillip sighed. Rachel knew that sigh. It meant that the old argument between her parents was starting again. "You're my wife. Your home is with me."

"I can take care of myself! I don't need you to—"

"Lower your voice. You'll upset Rachel."

"She might as well know the truth. It'll be a good lesson to find out what she's in for if she ever gets stupid and falls for a man! She'll end up in a cage like the big cats at the zoo—"

"Stop it, Lydia...."

"No! I won't stop. I'm sick of this city... the clattering of the trolley cars...all the people in the street! And that house... your mother. Your precious mother, who does everything right! Her perfect dinner parties where everybody sits. Talking in low voices. Clinking the glassware. Clink... Clink... Clink! I can't stand it anymore, Phillip. I want to go home!"

"We'll talk when we—"

"No! No! We'll talk now. Pull over. Pull over here..."

"When we get to the house, Lydia."

That rock-hard quality to her father's voice. How it must have scared the bad people when he made them go to jail.

Lydia grabbed for the steering wheel. "Now, I tell you! Here! Now!"

They wrestled. The car was swerving in wide, fishtail arcs down the center of the road.

In the back seat, the child Rachel held the box of pastries crushed against her chest as the car hit a greasy puddle and shot off the road into a cement piling. There was the horrible screaming of the tires, the bone-crushing slam of impact.

THE NEXT THING the child knew, she was curled in a ball on the floor between the back and front seats. The car was very still now, and the box pressed against her chest had burst. Grandmother Catherine wouldn't like it, not one bit. The sweet, sticky chocolate and whipped cream had ruined the frilly birthday dress she'd given her.

It was so quiet now, except for the creaking and groaning of the broken car around her and the hissing sound of steam escaping from somewhere under the hood.

"Mommy? Daddy?" the child called softly. No answer came.

Her head was aching. Bright spots danced and popped in front of her eyes. She felt her lids flutter and go lax as the wave of blackness engulfed her again.

"RACHEL? DEAR?" Gran's worried voice brought her back to the present.

Taking a long, fresh gulp of air, Rachel steadied herself against the railing, half expecting her mind to send her reeling back in time once again. But the seconds were passing; it became more certain that the storm of memory had played itself out for now.

"Rachel Diane, I'm so sorry...." Catherine was watching her helplessly.

"No, Catherine," she got out in a low tone. "I'm the one who needs to apologize. I don't know what got into me. I heard you mention Phillip and it ... set off a chain reaction, I guess."

"But for a moment there you looked so ..." Catherine cast about for the right words.

Rachel cut in before she could find them. "Why don't we just— Isn't there any coffee?"

Gran and Catherine exchanged sympathetic glances; Rachel pretended not to see.

"It needs warming. No, I'll do it. Sit down, dear. Watch the primroses bloom." Gran pulled herself from her chair and went inside.

Catherine gave Rachel an uncertain smile. "Do you think I ought to help?" That new consideration again; Catherine was offering Rachel a moment alone.

Rachel came away from the railing. Sitting down on the wooden boards at Catherine's feet, she gathered her long legs into her chin.

"No," she said softly. "Stay here with me. You've never seen the primroses bloom."

Catherine settled back in her chair. A silence that was almost companionable fell between them, broken only by the rush of water in the flume and the evensong of an occasional bird. Rachel felt the feather-light touch of a hand on her hair—hesitant, fleeting—before Gran returned to them with the steaming-hot coffee.

5

THE CABIN WAS STAINED a muted gray, the wood left in its natural state, rough to the touch. The gray made the structure blend into the surrounding trees, echoed the trunks of Douglas fir and black oak.

From the road the house seemed to be built into the hill above, so that the deck swung out on the air, supported by sturdy beams. But the winding drive behind revealed a large, clear space beside the single-car garage. Gideon's Model A and Chris's pickup had plenty of room to park.

Kane was waiting for them by the door, his hands in the pockets of a pair of tight-fitting black jeans. Johnny jumped down from the truck and ran up to him.

"We're here," he announced expansively. "I hope you got lots of food, because there's me and my Mom and my Dad and Cousin Rache and Granny Ethel and—"

"Slow down there, John," Chris called from the truck. "Kane'll change his mind about feedin' us." Sarah's curly head appeared as her husband took her hand and helped her to the ground.

"No way." Kane's rumbling laugh was warm. "I've got enough to feed an army."

"A whole army?"

"Well . . . almost."

Kane looked up from the earnest, small face to Rachel, who was coming toward him with Catherine on her arm. Rachel had taken more time than she would ever admit to with her appearance, choosing the rusty-gold silk blouse because she knew it caught the lights in her eyes and the burnt umber slacks for their trim, clinging fit. If his taunting remarks on the post office steps had forced her to take up the challenge and attend this erstwhile event, she might as well look her best.

"Kane, I'd like you to meet my... grandmother, Catherine Davis," Rachel said, to cover the shiver that fluttered through her at the appreciative gleam in his dark eyes. "Catherine, this is Kane Walker." Rachel didn't miss the slight lift of a silver eyebrow or the tiny, sly glance that darted once to Rachel and back to their tawny-haired host.

"It's good to meet you, Mrs. Davis." Somehow he made the timeworn phrase sound so honest, so very sincere.

The man could charm the pants off a nun, Rachel thought irreverently. Catherine's rosebud mouth bloomed up at the corners. She liked him—Rachel couldn't believe it. Catherine always reserved judgment on anyone until she'd known him or her for at least fifty years.

"We gonna stand here makin' polite noises and introducin' each other till dark, or you gonna show us inside, Kane Walker?" A crusty old cackle accompanied Gideon's question.

Offering Catherine his arm, Kane led them all into his house.

The kitchen-living area was all one room. Above was an open sleeping loft, cleverly divided by a sort of half partition into two bedrooms. The effect was of a cozy yet spare simplicity. Cedar trim and beams warmed the nubby-textured walls and ceiling. A big stone hearth graced one wall, and the love seat and two inviting chairs were covered in dove-gray corduroy.

Rachel drank in the magnificence of the oil painting over the fireplace. It was the Sierra Buttes at sunset, all stark grays and stunning purples. On the wall behind one of the corduroy chairs hung a grouping of wood-framed photographs. Rachel moved in for a closer look. She turned away quickly when the smiling face of Mariette Sayer looked back at her.

"These are lovely," Gran said, tracing the perfect, even seams on one of the bright quilted pillows stacked near the hearth.

"My Aunt Sandra made them," Kane said proudly.

"Your aunt?" Catherine's silver brow leaped upward. "Has she been to visit you here?"

"Not yet," Kane replied. "She lives in Lodi, not far from my folks."

"Then you are a Californian by birth," Catherine mused, as if she had made some wondrous discovery. "You aren't perhaps related to the Mendocino Walkers?"

Kane grinned. "I doubt it. My dad's family came out here from Oklahoma when he was a kid, hoping to make a new start in the land of milk and honey. They were dirt poor, with a lot of big dreams."

"And now?" Catherine asked, both silver brows lifted.

Kane shrugged. "My dad worked for the canneries, driving a truck, until he retired a few years ago."

"Kane here's a self-made man." Chris beamed. "What's the name of those health clubs? Circular Motion?"

"Centrifugal Force," Kane corrected. "That's the—"

"Force that tends to pull an object outward when it's rotating rapidly around a center," Gran concluded in schoolteacher tones.

Gideon raised his baseball cap just high enough to scratch his head. "Sometimes I feel like I'm hitchin' myself up to a walkin' dictionary."

Gran looked him right in the eye. "Perhaps you've had second thoughts."

"Heck, no!" Gideon patted her hand, which rested lightly on his arm. "A man with sense always falls for a woman who's smarter than him. Keeps him on his toes."

A warm pinkness crept upward on Gran's wrinkled cheeks. "Gideon Gentry," she said softly, "I do believe I'll keep you, after all."

Gideon gazed down at her in loving bemusement, then looked up to see that their fond exchange had been witnessed by all present. He cleared his throat. "Ah. Hmm. Yes. Centrifugal Force, eh? What's that got to do with keepin' in shape?"

"If you've got a week, I'll explain it to you," Kane replied.

Catherine's hand fluttered up to smooth her hair. "Surely you could give us a general idea," she encouraged sweetly.

Kane gave her a warm smile. "Actually, it's based on the concept that strength—and outward growth—occur once you find your center."

Gideon snorted. "Sounds real deep. But what does it mean?"

"If you're not careful," Kane warned, "I'll be forced to give you my introductory lecture."

"We're listenin'," Gideon challenged with his lopsided grin.

"Well—" Kane took a deep breath "—developing a fitness plan that's effective is a little like choosing a career or buying a home...or finding the person you want to spend your life with." His gaze lighted briefly on

Rachel. She kept her expression carefully noncommittal.

He went on. "You've got to consider what's going to work for you over a long period of time." Kane's lips curled in a rueful smile. "Unfortunately, most people give the whole process less thought than they would a blind date. They come in because their doctors told them to, or they want to look good in a bikini—reasons that are only going to last them till the doc stops nagging or summer's over and they can get back into those bulky sweaters and long pants.

"At Centrifugal Force, we try to center them down, work on making fitness an everyday part of their lives. We incorporate many of the more Eastern disciplines— yoga, meditation, t'ai chi ch'uan—to promote flexibility, concentration and balance. But we also include things like tennis and handball for people who need competition to get them motivated. And, of course, we provide Nautilus training and free weights. And we make sure we don't leave out a good aerobic workout—running or exercising to music—so the heart is strengthened—"

"Whoa!" Gideon guffawed. "I see what you mean about needing a week!"

"We try to set realistic goals," Kane continued, not missing a beat. "Each client gets an individual program designed especially for him—or her—taking into consideration things like age, life-style, the time they can reasonably afford to invest, any health problems they might have...."

Chris glanced down at his stomach, which in the past few years had developed a tendency to hang over his belt. "My major health problem is Sarah's cooking."

Kane looked at Gideon, his dark eyes bright with humor. "Had enough?"

"Sounds to me like you know what you're talkin' about," Gideon said with grudging respect. "But if it's all right with you, I'll stick to shovellin' snow in the winter, swimmin' in the summer and walkin' instead of ridin' whenever there's a choice."

"Hey—" Kane threw up a hand "—like I said, whatever works for you."

"Can I have a soda or somethin'?" Johnathan, clearly feeling left out and not liking it one bit, was tugging at a belt loop on Kane's black jeans.

"Mind your manners, Son," Chris chided.

"How about some lemonade?" Kane knelt and ruffled the little boy's dark hair. "Squeezed the lemons myself."

"Well, okay." Johnny trailed along behind as Kane went over to the refrigerator and brought out a big yellow pitcher. "It woulda been a lot easier to open a can. You don't got a can opener?"

"Don't *have* a can opener, Johnathan," Gran corrected as she followed the others out the glass doors onto the deck. Only Rachel hung back, lingering on the braid rug in front of the fireplace.

"Don't *have*," Johnny repeated obediently. "Well. Don't you *have* a can opener?"

Kane replied, straight-faced, that he did, but he liked his lemonade fresh.

An old Gibson guitar leaned up against the hearthstones. Rachel's pulse quickened as a vision of a slightly younger Kane assailed her.

He was sitting on the tousled blankets of the bed in her apartment in L.A., strumming the guitar, humming little snatches of melody as his wonderful, strong fingers danced across the strings. He was naked. And he held the guitar against his flat belly as he had held her only moments before—cherishingly, but with the demanding urgency of a hungry lover. She had crawled up behind him on the bed, kneaded the rippling thongs of muscle where his neck joined his shoulders. "Play me," she whispered.

"Again?" He laughed. Then he set the guitar aside and turned into her arms, to share with her another kind of music altogether.

Rachel blinked and shook her head, forcing her traitorous thoughts back to the present. But her hand came out of its own accord and plucked the E string. The single, mournful note echoed in the cheerful room.

Kane and Johnny were arranging glasses on a tray. At the sound from the guitar, the near-black eyes snared hers. A haunting tenderness moved at the corners of his mouth.

"Still writing songs?" Rachel asked, more to still the yearning inside her than to know the answer.

"Sometimes." A tiny muscle jerked in the sandpaper cheek and was still. "Big dreams, y'know." He turned his attention back to the tray.

"We could use some help, Cousin Rache," Johnny said. He obviously felt that whatever was going on between these grown-ups could wait until he'd had his lemonade.

"There's a bottle of Lachrima Christi up in that cabinet." Kane gestured to one of the cupboards.

He had remembered how she loved the wine. Lachrima Christi, Tears of Christ. They had drunk a whole bottle once. On a picnic in Griffith Park.

"My Daddy likes to have a beer," Johnny said.

Kane grinned down at him. "I've got it handled. There's a cooler out on the deck."

"What's for dessert?" Johnny asked, then amended, "I always get dessert if I eat my whole dinner."

Kane pointed to a blue bucket with a detachable knob of a motor and a cord bearing a plug at the end.

"Homemade ice cream."

"That makes ice cream?" Johnny looked doubtful.

"It's electric," Kane explained. "But it's not exactly the latest model. Makes a lot of racket, to tell you the truth. We'll hook it up out in front so we won't have to listen to it grinding away."

"What kind?"

"Electric."

"No. The ice cream."

"Strawberry. Fresh strawberry."

Johnny turned the flavor over in his mind. "That's my favorite," he decided at last.

Rachel found the corkscrew and opened the bottle of wine. The scent of it was heady. She rolled the rubbery cork in her palm—just the right touch of moisture. Beyond the window over the sink, a blue jay serenaded a squirrel from the branches of a live oak. The squirrel sat up on his hind legs, sniffed disdainfully and scampered away.

The wine, the homemade ice cream—Kane must have made a special trip to Grass Valley to buy the strawberries. The more popular California wines were all that lined the shelves of Jim's Market in Downieville. Their host had gone out of his way to make the evening a success.

When Rachel took her place at the picnic table on the deck, a long black-clad thigh slid in next to her. Kane reached for the wine bottle and filled her glass, then his own.

"To all those Italian peasants and their busy, stomping feet." He clinked his glass against hers. "You still have that one dimple in that funny place below your mouth when you smile."

"Pass the salad, please."

The steaks were tender, barbecued to a slightly charred, medium-rare perfection by Kane and Gideon. They had corn on the cob and baked potatoes smothered in butter and sour cream and a large spinach salad with a vinaigrette dressing.

The sweep of hip and thigh so close, rubbing against her as Kane passed her the butter or reached for the salt, kept Rachel from giving the hearty meal the attention it deserved. Though she was careful never to stare at him directly, Rachel allowed herself, more than once, a sideways glance from under the veil of her lashes.

She couldn't help but note the easy warmth that flowed from him, making her family feel at home. He listened attentively to Gran's detailed instructions for the care and maintenance of a sourdough starter and laughed uproariously with the rest at Gideon's tales of his early years as a pilot in the Alaskan bush. Yet in spite of the ever-present Walker charm, there was still a brooding quality about Kane. That quality hadn't completely disappeared, Rachel decided, but it had mellowed somewhat. His sense of humor was more easily roused, his response to the ebb and flow of conversation around him less guarded. It was as if the years had taught him something of the ephemeral nature of life and happy moments like these, as if he knew he must embrace them fully, for they were bound to slip away.

"Couldn't eat another bite if my life depended on it," Chris said, ruefully surveying the two remaining steaks on the big platter nearby.

"You should take your own advice more often." Sarah patted her husband's stomach playfully. "People will begin to wonder which one of us is having the baby."

"Don't hound me, woman! What else is there in life but good food and good friends—" Chris tweaked his wife's button nose affectionately "—and the love of a good woman?" He bent his head and placed a light kiss on Sarah's happily flushed cheek.

The sweep of corded thigh at Rachel's side brushed lightly once again. She rose a little awkwardly, extricating herself from the narrow space between bench and table.

"Let's just . . . take these things inside."

Kane clasped her arm gently. The touch sent a message to the lobes of her ears and turned them blushing pink.

"You're going to lose your fork," he said, and broke the contact to nudge her fork back on the plate she clutched so tightly.

Everyone pitched in to help clear the table, and soon they sat about the deck scooping up cold sweet ice cream, tasting delightfully of fresh strawberries, into their eager mouths. Rachel noted with a smile that Chris didn't refuse a second helping.

The Evening Star twinkled more and more brightly as night came on.

Star light, star bright,
First star I see tonight.
I wish I may, I wish I might
Have this wish I wish tonight.

After reciting, Johnny closed his eyes very tightly for a moment, then looked up at his mother.

"Do you think I'll get it, Mommy?"

"Time will tell," said his mother mysteriously as she gathered him more closely into the crook of her arm.

"I noticed the guitar inside," Catherine said. "Will you play us a tune, Kane?"

Kane raked a hand through his hair. Rachel grinned at the gesture. She used to accuse him of not owning a comb. "Well, I . . ."

Rachel took another sip of the wine. An inchoate note of longing vibrated through her. She wanted to hear him play again. "Please, Kane." Her eyes met his directly now.

"Please what?" he teased softly, reminding her of those moments at the Cliffs a week ago.

"Would you play for us?" There. She had told him what she wanted; it hadn't been so hard.

He rose from his seat with that familiar, sinuous grace, strode into the house and returned to them with the guitar. He sat back down on the bench next to Rachel. Long fingers moved swiftly over the strings, tuning them with a sure and practiced touch.

"What an interesting ring," Catherine remarked cryptically. "What kind of stone is that?"

"Smoky quartz. It was a gift. I was told it matched my eyes."

"Hmm . . ." said Catherine.

"Anybody know 'Baby What You Do When You Do Me Like That'?" Kane asked.

"Never heard of it," Gideon drawled.

"I'm not surprised. Wrote it myself. I wanted to be a rock 'n' roll star once. Gave it up for my health."

Gran chuckled. "Play a few bars. Maybe we can pick it up."

Gideon cackled a little at this. Gran nudged him in the ribs. It was no secret that Gideon's bride-to-be was notoriously tone deaf.

"It goes like this." Kane pounded out a rollicking melody on the hapless guitar.

Baby what you do when
you do me like that.
My teeth are in my toes
and my stomach's in my hat.

I don't know how you do it
but you sure can do it good.
I guess I shouldn't tell you
but I surely wish you would.

"Would what?" Chris laughed.

"Guess we'll have to compose another verse to find out." Kane's white teeth flashed in a broad grin.

A riotous half hour went by while everyone suggested new verses to the song. Then they switched to old standards, Kane's deep, firm voice leading them, Rachel's singing harmony.

It was well past ten o'clock when Chris glanced at his sleeping son, who was curled up in a lounge chair with a jacket of Kane's wrapped around him for a blanket. "Time we were headin' down the road," Chris said.

"One more song." The words were out of Rachel's mouth before she could stop them. It was so lovely here with her family close around her. They had been singing old spirituals, and the haunting melodies on the Sierra night seemed to weave a spell, one it was surely too soon to break.

But Gran and Gideon were already on their feet. Chris was taking his sleeping son in his arms.

"Catherine and I want to attend the early service tomorrow," Gran said somewhat regretfully. "It's been a wonderful evening. I thank you, Kane."

"I hope you'll come again." Kane turned to Rachel. "If you want to stay for a while, I'll drive you down."

She knew she should say no, that four hours ago she'd been trundling across the small bridge on Goodyears Creek Road in Gideon's Model A, steeling herself for an evening she had wanted to avoid. But it had all turned to magic somehow. The inviting simplicity of the cabin, the Tears of Christ, the old guitar. His sure fingers still knew how to find the melodies, lifting her to a place where her mind could not hear any warning signal.

"Stay, dear, if you'd like." Gran put her arm through Gideon's.

"I think I will—just for a while."

Kane saw his guests to the door. Rachel remained on the deck, resting her chin on her arms as she leaned against the railing.

A single shadow of a cloud floated like the most gossamer of fabrics across the silver globe that was the moon. The crickets, shy of daylight, were weaving high, chirping trills of song now that the seductive night had charmed them out. Below her on the road, the headlights of Chris's pickup cut the dark, disappearing soon around a bend, only to be followed by the skewed lamps of Gideon's Model A. Then the old car was swallowed up, too, by the blackness of the trees.

Rachel heard the glass door slide open behind her, but she didn't turn. She sensed rather than heard Kane's step as he came to lean on the railing beside her. They gazed upon the stars and moon together, not touching. But in some deeper place they shared an intimacy, sheltering and yet as open as the thick curtain of stars over their heads.

"Who who who,' asked an owl from a black oak, so close by that they heard the hollow flutter of his wings as he took flight, revealing himself for a moment before he disappeared into a stand of pines below the road. *Is the sharing of silence a healing thing*, Rachel wondered. Tonight, at that moment, it seemed it could be.

Utterly without guile, she turned her eyes upon the man beside her. The clean outline of his profile, sheened silver by the pale light from above, tugged at some tender place within her.

Don't get too close. Such feelings are dangerous, the old, familiar warning voice inside her said. But the voice was far away now, muted by the scent of cedar and the joyful, abandoned symphony of the crickets.

"When I was a kid, we read about the gold rush and the towns that sprang up from nowhere all over the Sierra foothills. I saw a picture in a history book. It was a cabin on a hill. The caption underneath said, 'It's difficult to believe that this idyllic setting was once overrun with desperate men whose blood ran hot with gold fever.'" Kane chuckled, ruefully. "I memorized the caption. I had to look up 'idyllic.' That was probably the only time I used a dictionary on purpose during the whole of my formative years."

He picked up a twig that had fallen on the railing and broke it in half, then broke the half in half. His eyes didn't leave the shadowed trees. "That picture seemed a long way from Lodi."

"It's not so very far," Rachel said, watching his hands as they snapped the twig.

He tossed the tiny sections away from him and turned to her. "It's far enough." The naked hunger in his eyes startled her. Without realizing it, she jerked back from him an inch. She felt his urge to take hold of her, just as a second later she felt him quell it. He clenched one hand, tapped it ineffectually on the railing, then forced his gaze back out onto the night. "Sometimes, Rachel . . ." The tortured whisper was too much for her to let him bear alone. She raised two fingers and placed them on his lips. "Shh. . . ."

"But I want you to know. . . ." The warmth of his breath against her hand stirred the waiting fires within her. She moved to him of her own accord, drawing the tawny head to her lips with a sureness that surprised her. "Oh, my woods witch," he murmured against her parted mouth, "you shouldn't start what you're not prepared to finish." But his tongue darted in, catching hers and claiming it, while his arms went around her, molding her softness to his hard length.

She ran clutching hands along the moving sinews of his back, wishing only that by some miracle she would never have to let him go. Her blood was a pounding current, a river of desire. It beat so hard against the cruel dam that had held it back too long. . . .

She thrust her eager tongue between his teeth, tasting the sweet and salt beyond his lips, then withdrew enough to lay a trail of tiny kisses along the firm jaw to his ear.

With a strangled groan he buried his face in her hair, raking his fingers through the dark mass as if he would wrap them both forever in the silken web of curls.

"I want you, Rachel. God help me, I've always wanted you." He grasped her chin in the cup of his hands and looked deeply into her eyes, as if by the sheer force of his need he could wrest some unknown answer from her.

Rachel didn't have an answer, just a hunger of her own that ran like molten fire along her nerves whenever this man touched her. "I don't know," she said helplessly. "I don't know anything when you touch me. . . ." *Or when you look at me like that*, she added silently.

His spiky lashes lowered to the pulse that pounded in the satin place where her neck met the rusty gold of her shirt. Then his hands were there, running sure as a promise down to the first button, tugging it from the hole, then on to the next. He spread the silken fabric, laid his lips to the gently swelling cleft between the full mounds of her breasts.

"Oh, God. How I've dreamed . . . dreamed . . ." His words were lost in the laving wetness of his tongue. He smoothed the transparent lace of her bra aside to find her nipple, taking it into his mouth, running little circles around it until she feared it would burst with wanting more, more. . . .

But he had lifted his head again, was staring deeply into her eyes, seeking again that answer when she didn't know the question. The wild song of the crickets swirled to a plateau, pulsing still, not daring to go higher. The ragged urgency of her own breath caught on a strangled sigh of loss, then tangled in the cloudy mass of her hair as she laid her head against his chest.

"Are you sure, Rachel?" His heart thudded like a hammer against her ear, pounding, hollow waves of sound, slowing now at the command of his will alone.

She wouldn't answer, couldn't answer. She turned her lips to the fabric of his shirt, scented, as he was, of musty evergreen, and mouthed the sculptured flesh beneath.

With a feral groan he grabbed her close once more. Greedy hands ran down the swelling contours of her hips, then up to her waist, where he grasped her slimness and set her back from him. "Inside." With a curt nod he indicated the glass doors. Taking her hand, he led her through them.

He left her on the braided oval of the rug and flicked on the lamp beside a chair. She waited, the rushing fire within her licking hungry tongues of flame at every nerve. Why didn't he come back to her?

He sat down in the chair, the steely muscles of his legs defined so clearly beneath the black cloth of his jeans. The hard swelling told her of his need. Why didn't he come back to her? A darkness shuttered his eyes.

"I don't want to be used. Not again, Rachel. I won't make love to you until you admit that there's more than sex between us."

Her eyes darted away from his, suddenly wide and frightened as those of a doe caught on a mountain road by an oncoming rush of headlights. She saw the wood-framed photograph that hung on the wall behind him, a group of smiling people all wearing T-shirts with a bright, mandala logo.

The mandala, the wheel of life, she thought, her mind confused, snatching at random impressions to get her bearings now that the coiling spring of desire had snapped. *In the center of the mandala it says Centrifugal Force*, she told herself. *And the smiling people work for him. All except the woman standing next to him in the picture—the one with her arm through his. That's Mariette.*

How could she have forgotten Mariette? Mariette of the violet eyes. Well into her forties, with a daughter who must be almost grown now, but still possessed of a youthful, fresh-complexioned beauty. And such a good businesswoman—not only a powerful force in the social politics of Hollywood moviemaking, but also the woman who had seen the potential in Kane Walker. Kane Walker, who now sat staring at Rachel as she waited like a fool with her blouse undone before the unlit fire in his cabin on a hill.

Shaking, angry fingers shoved the buttons back into their holes.

"It's too soon, isn't it?"

How dare he adopt that patronizing tone? "Too soon?" She spat the words out. "Don't you talk to me about 'too soon'! It's too late, and you know it. It's been too late for six years!"

"It's better that you run from me now than after—"

"There isn't going to be any after. Never. Not ever again." Angry tears threatened to spill the boundaries of her lashes and humiliate her more. "But that wouldn't bother you. You've always had plenty of willing partners to choose from."

His voice was weary. "You've told yourself that lie for so long now, I imagine you might even believe it." He rose from the chair and went to the glass door, snapping it shut with an air of finality. "I belong to you. Just as you belong with me. All I'm afraid of is that I'll be older than Gideon before you find that out."

"No . . ." she whispered. He shot her a glance, surprised at the fear in the single, low exclamation. "I . . . I don't belong to anyone," she finished. She was trembling.

"Come on," he said with a gentleness that startled her. "I'll drive you home."

6

SLEEP WAS ELUSIVE that night. Rachel lay in her single bed under the eaves staring up at the slanted, bare-beamed ceiling. Because of the wine, she told herself, the calculated kindness he had shown her family, the aching familiarity of his practiced hands on the strings of the old guitar.

Rachel clenched her hands under the smooth sheets. He had toyed with her, stirred the embers of a fire better left cold, then announced that *he* didn't want to be used! She rolled over and buried her head in her pillow. Had tonight been some kind of cruel revenge? Some carefully orchestrated humiliation for that time when he'd come to her after she had told him it was over?

Rachel clenched her fists more tightly, feeling her nails carving half-moons into her palms, hoping the sharp, localized pain would keep her mind from conjuring up the past.

But her effort was wasted. Her mind had turned traitor, as it had too often these past few days. Something inside her insisted on dredging up the very memories she wanted most to forget....

AFTER THAT DISASTROUS CONFRONTATION at Mariette's party, Kane had tried to reach Rachel several times. She hadn't returned his calls, had in fact left her answering machine on round the clock so she wouldn't have to talk to him. But that hadn't stopped him. In the darkest hours between midnight and dawn, he had pounded on her door.

"Go away. I don't want—"

"Let me in."

"It's late."

"You're damn right it's late. I want to talk to you."

"You have no right."

"Open this door, Rachel. Or your neighbors are going to get one damn fine show." His angry whisper told her he would carry out his threat. She fumbled with the lock. He shoved back the door and was inside.

His shorts and T-shirt were stained with sweat. The honey hair clung to his forehead, damp and spiky. Had he been running—at 2:00 a.m.? She clutched the facings of her robe together; he would know she was naked underneath.

"Is there something wrong with your phone? Can you believe I've been getting the same message for four days now?" The heavy sarcasm was made dangerous by the silky lowness of his tone, the ragged intake of his breath.

She had no words for him. Blindly she struck out, slapping at his face with her open palms. He grabbed both her wrists and pinned them behind her. The scent of him swam around her.

Somehow their lips were crushed together and the silken wisp of robe had fallen to the floor. It was a battle, then, not love. It took place where they fell, a tangle of seeking limbs and mouths, by the door. When she cried out her completion, the sound was animal in her ears, a wild scream of the female, triumphant at the kill. His own release came soon after.

They collapsed against each other in a fearful stillness broken only by the torn sound of slowing breath and the tiny flipping of the seconds on the digital clock on the wall. He moaned against her throat. She wanted to pull him closer then. To stroke the damp hair at his temples, to soothe away his pain. Instead she shoved him off her and struggled to her feet, grabbing the balled-up robe against her for protection.

"Get out."

He rolled over, laid an arm across his eyes as if he couldn't bear to look at her above him. The lax surrender of the powerful male body at her feet made her long to reach for him again—to warm him with her woman's strength—to heal and make things right. "Mariette may enjoy this kind of treatment. But it's really not my style." She made her voice flat. Hard.

One moment he was sprawled across the floor—the next he seemed to tower above her. His magnificent form was taut as a bowstring, his eyes black holes of flame.

"Leave Mariette out of this."

"How can I? She's your—"

"My friend." He cut her off. "And my business partner."

"Oh, she's your partner, all right. Just like all those other bored, rich bitches who can't get enough of the Kane Walker system for total physical fitness!"

The holes of flame bored through her, burned down to her deepest core and found her wanting. If seconds before she had been afraid of his tight-held rage, now she felt the cutting edge of his scorn. "I knew you were jealous, Rachel. But I never believed you'd allow yourself to think of me as some kind of . . . whore." The ugly word came out on a tortured breath. "Can't you see it's all for you? I know you'll never take me seriously until I can offer you more than my songs and my dreams."

"I don't want what you're offering," she countered scathingly.

"I don't understand . . ."

"Just let me alone!" she cried desperately. "I . . . I want my freedom! To be free of you!"

"I've put no chains on you. Rachel, I—"

"Will you please . . . just . . . go."

He gathered up his clothes and dressed. The silence between them was as thick as any wall. "You can start answering your phone again," he said at last. "You'll get no more calls from me." Then he was gone.

TWO DAYS LATER the envelope came in the mail. There was no return address. Inside were the lyrics to a song.

Not yet morning when I left you,
  locked behind your wall of dreams . . .

Tearing it up had done no good. The words were burned on her memory like a brand.

"Enough. Enough of the past," Rachel muttered to herself. Sitting up, she switched on the lamp by the bed and stole a glance at the clock: 2:00 a.m.

Her palms ached dully. By clenching them so tightly, she had actually drawn blood.

Rachel squeezed her eyes shut, but still another image rose unbidden and flashed clearly on the inside of her lids: Kane's broad back as he walked out her door that last time. His shirt had been spotted with dark stains. Blood. In the passionate struggle on the floor of her apartment, her nails had drawn blood.

Rachel flung back the covers and brought her feet to the floor. Her eyes felt grainy and swollen. With the backs of her hands she rubbed at them.

Behind her she heard a low moan. It came from beyond the partition that separated the room Rachel slept in from the spare bedroom where Catherine lay. Was her father's mother having a nightmare? Listening more closely, she recognized the sounds of a troubled sleep. Was Catherine, like her granddaughter, haunted by painful memories tonight?

Rachel massaged her temples, noticing again the drops of blood, sticky and clotting now, on her palms. They needed rinsing. Cool water would soothe them, and a couple of aspirin would ease her pounding head.

Rising, she tiptoed to the half bath stuck under the eaves at the top of the stairs. She didn't bother to switch on the light but tossed the aspirin down in the dark, washing them past her dry throat with water she bent to suck directly from the faucet. Then she rinsed her hands, sighing as the liquid coolness took away the hurt. She avoided confronting her dim reflection in the glass above the sink and crept back to her bed as quickly as she'd come.

With the bedside light off again and the room in darkness, she punched at her pillow, trying to get comfortable, trying vainly to sleep. On the other side of the partition Catherine still tossed and moaned, the box springs beneath her complaining with her every move.

A woman's moan. Heard from beyond a wall. It reminded Rachel of— "No!" Rachel bit her lip as she realized she'd uttered the single syllable out loud. She wrapped her pillow around her head in a childish effort to hide from the images that had found her again. . . .

IN THE HOUSE in San Francisco, Rachel's bedroom had been next to her parents'. Often, late at night, she would hear strange sounds beyond the wall, wonder vaguely at the nature of the moans and funny sighs Lydia made, worry that Phillip must be hurting her.

Some nights they would argue in muffled tones before the moaning started. The voices would always be carefully low pitched, but charged with an urgency that frightened a young child.

Though Rachel knew spying was wrong, there were times when she couldn't help herself—she laid her ear to the wall.

"I can't stay here. Please, Phillip. Just let me . . ."

"I need you. Here. With me."

"I'm dying here. Can't you see you're killing me?"

"How do I kill you? Like this . . . and this?"

"Don't . . . don't do that."

"Love me, Liddy. It'll be all right."

"It can't be all right. Never. This is not my life. I can't be what you want!"

"Your life!" The springs creaked in her parents' bed. Angry feet paced the floor beyond the wall. "You want to hide from life—hide in your beat-up clothes with your hair a mess, wandering around the hills by yourself, searching for something that's right here with me!"

"There's nothing here with you. Your mother hates me. She hates me, Phillip. She knows I'm all wrong for you."

"That's not true."

"Yes, it is. And she's right. Do you hear me? She's right. You need a wife who cares about the things you do. A wife who charms and flatters and watches your back at cocktail parties. A wife who gets her hair done regularly and takes care of her nails. I'm not her. I could never be her."

"Then who exactly are you, Liddy?"

"I don't know. Some kind of . . . throwback, I guess. A pioneer with no frontiers left to conquer. Born a century too late, born a woman on top of that."

"And you think there's some way you can travel back in time, to an era where things were more to your liking? And while you're at it, do you figure you'll change yourself into a man? It won't work, Liddy. You're all woman. That's one thing I'm sure of."

"I was only nineteen when we got married. I hadn't had time to work things out in my life. But I know . . . I can do it. I'll find work that's . . . useful. And not in the city."

"Far away from me, you mean."

"Phillip. You belong here. I don't. There's only one place we have anything in common. And that...doesn't last. If I stay, what will I do when you start looking elsewhere?"

"That's not going to happen."

"It will. Eventually. You'll meet a woman—an attractive woman—who wants the same things you want. And you'll wonder what you ever saw in me. By that time it'll be too late for me. I'll have nothing but you, and then you'll be gone, too."

Her father was protesting again, but the child drew her head back from the wall, feeling confused and bewildered by the strange talk of grown-ups.

Oh, she shouldn't have spied. If she hadn't spied, she wouldn't have to know that Grandmother Catherine hated Lydia, or that Daddy was going to get a new wife.

She was just about to curl back under the covers and tell herself that what she had heard was all a bad dream, when the sound of her own name caught her up short. She pressed her ear to the wall again.

"What about Rachel?" her father was saying. "Have you considered your daughter? Do you imagine I'll let you drag her off to the hills with you again?"

"You can keep her if you want." Lydia's voice was utterly flat. "Catherine can raise her. Catherine's a much better mother than I've ever been. You said so yourself."

"Rachel needs—"

"Rachel, Rachel. Always Rachel. You've thrown her in my face one too many times. It's not going to work anymore. She'll have to learn soon enough what life is all about. Let her start now. I want my freedom, Phillip. One way or another, I'm going to get it."

"Is that all? Is that all you want, Liddy?"

More creakings of the bed as her father's weight descended back upon it. They must be fighting now. Rachel could hear the strange moans and funny sighs. If Lydia won, would she get freedom?

"No. Let me . . . Phillip, please . . ."

"You belong to me. I'll never let you go."

"No, Phillip. I . . . I don't belong to anyone. . . ."

"I DON'T BELONG TO ANYONE . . ." the grown-up Rachel mouthed the words again, knowing they were the same ones she'd repeated to Kane just hours ago.

The memory of spying on her parents' midnight battles was hard to deal with; it had stayed safely locked in her subconscious for more than twenty years. It made her feel guilty—and almost as confused as her child self had been.

From the other side of the partition in her grandmother's house, there was only silence now. Catherine must have settled into more peaceful slumber.

Rachel felt her own body relaxing, not sure how she knew it but oddly content that her mind was through toying with her for the night. Sighing gratefully, she turned on her side and drifted off into much-needed sleep.

THE NEXT FEW DAYS passed quickly. Rachel had a lot to do orchestrating her plans for the coming wedding. She was foiling Gran at every turn, making sure the folding tables never arrived from the town hall in Downieville, calling the ladies of the Community Club from the phone booth by the schoolhouse to tell them she was surprising her grandmother and planning to do all the decorations herself. Could they spread the word? Make excuses if Gran requested their help in setting up?

It had been necessary to take Catherine into her confidence. Her father's mother had smiled, delighted, and set about keeping Gran as busy as possible with other things. The silk-blend suit Catherine had planned to wear to the wedding just wouldn't do at all. She wanted to buy something special. And she would be deeply honored if Ethel would accompany her to choose just the right dress. And what did Ethel plan to wear? "But Ethel, you wore that last Sunday. It's lovely, yes. But— Oh. I've just thought what my gift to you will be. I want to buy your dress. We'll choose it together. We'll drive down to Sacramento first thing tomorrow— Don't worry about the tables, Rachel will see to them. And we can pick up the paper plates and plastic flatware on the way, if we remember." Rachel grinned. Trust Catherine to conveniently forget and be clever enough to keep Gran from bringing it up until it was too late.

The food was to be provided as Gran had planned it; each guest would bring a favorite dish. The Community Club members called daily, signing up for a vegetable souffle or a salad mold. Gran kept a list so the menu would have a little of everything. But when she asked Ruth Daniels or Mary Short if either could loan her a nice linen tablecloth—well, suddenly the ladies just had to get off the phone.

Gran was more than a little frazzled by Friday morning. She was banging pots and pans around when Rachel came down the stairs at 7:00 a.m. "You can tone it down, Gran. I think the dead people in the graveyard up the hill are awake now."

"I'm getting married tomorrow. And nothing is ready. No one is helping. That cousin of yours promised he'd have the tables here yesterday. I haven't the faintest idea where I'm going to get the paper plates we need, unless I give in and pay an arm and a leg for them in town!

"Mary Short is wonderful with flower arrangements, but she'd rather talk about her cherry pies. I have cherry pies! I have all the food we could possibly eat in a hundred years arriving from all over the county, and I have nothing to put it on!" Gran sank into a chair.

Rachel was at the coffeepot, lifting it to pour herself a cup. She set the pot down and went to Gran, wrapping her arms around the slumped shoulders from behind.

Rachel had wanted only to make magic, to present her grandmother with a fairy-tale setting for her wedding party. She had known her scheme would frustrate Gran, but she hadn't let herself admit how much.

"I'm sorry," Rachel said softly.

"Thank you, but that doesn't solve my problem. I need help, not apologies."

"I . . . I wanted to surprise you. I have the decorations all planned. There'll be a truck arriving in a few hours. It'll have the tables and the plates and everything else we need, as well as three of my best people to set up."

Gran sniffed. Rachel reached for a tissue from the box on the windowsill and handed it to her. "You should have told me," Gran said.

"I know. I just . . ."

Gran shook her head. "Never in all my seventy-nine years have I spent such a week as the one just past." Gran pulled the bifocals from the end of her nose and rubbed at them with the tissue.

Rachel gave her another quick hug. "Don't be angry with me."

"I don't want anything fancy," Gran warned as she settled her glasses against the bridge of her nose. "Just to share our happiness with our friends. It's to be a simple gathering of—"

Rachel laughed. "I promise, Gran. No naked dancing girls. No drunken revelers swinging from the chandeliers."

"I have no chandeliers." Gran was chuckling now. "It looks like you've had the best of me. Let this be a lesson to you."

"A lesson to me?" Rachel asked, bewildered.

"Yes. Never be sure things will go as you intended. Someone you love may have other plans." Gran gave a crisp little nod, as if she had just tied the secret of the universe into a neat bundle. "Now. What time did you say that truck was due to arrive?"

KELLY AND MAX PULLED UP in the station wagon at a little after ten. The truck was nowhere in sight. Rachel ran down the steps to greet them.

"Where's the truck?"

Max looked at Kelly. Kelly cast a glance toward heaven. "A person could lose her lunch on some of those turns." Kelly groaned. "Why didn't you warn us?"

"The truck?"

"I can see she really missed us," Max said. "We're not even out of the car yet, and all the boss wants to know is—"

"Where's the truck?" Rachel demanded again. She found herself giggling when her two employees mouthed the words with her.

Max shot his thumb back over his shoulder. "Up at the top of that ridge back there, before you hit that ninety-degree grade that leads to the single-car-width bridge."

"Up the cut?" Rachel asked.

"I don't know what you call it," Kelly replied. "But Carlos calls it dangerous. He says to remind you he's too young to die, and he refuses to come down until someone can prove to him beyond a reasonable doubt that he'll be able to make that turn that leads to the bridge."

"It looks worse than it is. Logging rigs used to do it all the time," Rachel explained coaxingly. "It's true," she protested, at Max's derisive snort.

Gideon, who had arrived only moments before, came to her rescue. "Guess I'll have to hightail it up there and save another quiverin' flatlander, eh, gal?" He cackled, throwing an arm around Rachel and grinning down at her. "Nice to meet you folks." He tipped his baseball cap at Max and Kelly and ambled off toward the bridge.

"Who's thay-at?" Kelly asked in a fair imitation of Gideon's drawl.

Rachel shrugged. "The bridegroom, of course."

The huge semi and single-car trailer with Illusions Unlimited painted in the shape of an opalescent rainbow across its sides made it down the cut without mishap. Before they began unloading, Gran departed with Gideon to spend the night at Chris's. "Are you sure you can manage without me?" Gran asked Rachel doubtfully as Gideon herded her toward the Model A.

"Gran. I do this for a living, remember?"

"You'll have to get that truck off the street soon. It's blocking traffic."

"We'll unload the big stuff now and park it out in the flat across from Riley's."

Gran looked unconvinced. "I feel a little guilty. . . ."

Rachel gave an exasperated sigh. "Are you going to let me do this or aren't you?"

The network of wrinkles fanned out like the rays of the sun as Gran smiled. "It appears I don't have a choice," she said, and climbed into the Model A. Gideon put the car in gear, and they wheezed off toward the bridge.

Carlos hooked his thumbs into the belt loops of his faded jeans and ambled over. "Well, Boss. You ready to make a little magic for your grandma on her wedding day?"

"I'm ready." Rachel nodded. "Let's get to work."

Catherine helped Kelly with the arrangements of wildflowers and pine boughs while Rachel directed Max and Carlos in unloading the heavy stuff from the truck. The Community Club had donated the use of the schoolhouse, so the folding tables were set up inside for the buffet. Rachel worked from a large blueprint of her design, and each bare table had a smaller blueprint taped to it showing the placement of centerpiece, serving dishes, silverware and glassware.

A public address system with tape deck and speakers had to be put together out in the school yard, along with a small bandstand where the four-piece group from the Fireman's Ball would play. Paper lanterns depicting gold rush scenes were hung on wires from tree to tree. Strings of tiny lights were woven among the branches.

Fiberglass chairs and tables, specially designed to look like carved-out tree trunks and flat-topped boulders, were arranged in conversational groups around Gran's yard. More lights had to be wrapped around the posts and railings of porches and eaves.

It was late afternoon when they ran out of masking tape. Rachel called to Kelly, who was in the house at the kitchen table with Catherine, wiring the stems of some of the more delicate flowers.

"Five rolls!" wailed Kelly. "Elaine and I were both sure it would be enough!"

"Relax," Rachel said. "Things have been going too smoothly, anyway. I was beginning to get nervous."

"I'll go," said Carlos. "Where's the mall?" His face split in a broad grin.

Rachel wrinkled her nose at him. "The nearest shopping mall is sixty miles from here."

His eyes widened in pretended shock. "No mall? I thought you said we were still in California."

Rachel laughed. "You guys take a break. I'll run into town and be back in an hour. Catherine, do you think you can find something for these starving slaves of mine to eat?"

"I think I can manage," Catherine said from the front steps. She carried a wild rose in one hand and a small section of wire in the other. A warm flood of tenderness washed over Rachel. Was this the cold, aloof woman who had intimidated her so for twenty-nine years? "Come inside, you three." Catherine gestured with the rose. "I'll burn you some grilled-cheese sandwiches."

"How old is she?" asked Kelly when Catherine had disappeared into the house.

"Eighty-one in September."

"Amazing," Kelly marveled, and followed Max and Carlos inside.

Kane's Land Rover was near the playground when Rachel pulled into the parking lot by the fire-bell tower. Did that mean he was up there? Or would she run into him on the street?

After her sleepless night following the barbecue, Rachel had done quite well in pushing him out of her mind. If smoky quartz eyes had more than once invaded her dreams, the days had been too busy for brooding over her actions of that night or over his baffling rejection of her.

Did he no longer desire her? The possibility stung more than her pride. Her physical need for him had never been entirely vanquished. Sometimes it was still an aching void that nothing in her otherwise satisfying life could fill. She had let herself believe he felt the same. It was a cold comfort, but one she had depended on.

What was he doing up in the school yard? Shooting baskets? Or had he talked someone—maybe that redhead who had hung all over him at the Fireman's Ball—into a game of tennis? Rachel took a few hesitant steps toward the chain-link fence that surrounded the playground before she caught herself and headed up Main Street.

Sierra Hardware had all the masking tape she needed. Rachel bought five more rolls to be on the safe side, along with some extra staples for the staple gun. There was a lot of extension cord to hook up, and it would need to be secured against walls and tree trunks, out of the way of traffic.

She stopped in at the Sugar Plum Confectionery for a mint-chip ice cream cone, deciding to sit under the firebell tower to enjoy her treat.

The Land Rover was still there. It would be nice to be in the shade. There was that lovely weeping willow just inside the playground. She could sit there. The afternoon had grown quite warm. Licking the sides of the sweet green stuff to keep it from melting all over her fingers, she wandered up toward the gate.

He was shooting baskets. Dribbling the ball with such smoothness that it seemed he had a magnet connected to his hand. The soaring arc of his arm as he tossed the ball into the ring above was beautiful to behold. Rachel sat down on the bench beneath the willow and watched him for a time, polishing off the last of her ice cream cone. When he saw her, he pretended to stumble so that the ball got away from him. It rolled across the blacktop and stopped at the toes of her blue espadrilles. He loped over to retrieve it.

Wiping away a bead of perspiration that had escaped the sweatband around his head, he knelt and scooped the ball smoothly into his palm. "Shopping?" he asked, indicating the brown bag beside her on the bench.

"We ran out of tape. Masking tape. For the setup. We thought we had enough, but we didn't—have enough. Tape, I mean." She was stuttering like a sixteen-year-old on her first date. What in the world had possessed her to follow him up here? "I . . . bought an ice cream cone. I thought it would be nice to sit here. Under the willow—while I ate it."

"Was it?"

"What?"

"Nice."

"Oh. Nice. Yes. I used to sit here all the time. To think."

"About what?" He was lowering his glistening, powerful frame into the space beside her. A trickle of moisture escaped from behind his ear and ran down to the crew neck of his shirt, where it disappeared. "You're doing it again."

"What?"

"Chewing your bottom lip."

"About the other night . . ."

He captured both her hands and turned them palm up. "Your lifeline is broken in the middle." He traced the feathery line with a finger. "This could mean many things."

"Such as?"

"You will die and come back to life."

"And?"

"You have two lives."

"What else?"

His head was bent over her hand. She resisted the urge to lay her lips on the damp hair. Her pulse accelerated; she could feel it beating like a caged bird against the smooth skin of her neck.

"You will find what you've been seeking and the rest of your time on this earth will be drastically altered."

Rachel cleared her throat and gently pulled her hands away. He leaned back against the bench. Two children, a boy and a girl, were playing on the swings side by side. Rachel could hear them challenging each other: "I can go higher than you can!" Didn't they know that if you went too high you would turn inside out?

"I didn't know you were a fortune teller, too."

"That will be seventy-five cents."

"You have so many talents."

"And I thought you hadn't noticed."

"Do you ever . . . regret giving up your music?"

"Feeling guilty? I seem to remember telling you once that I did it all for you." She flushed deeply.

"Listen to me, Rachel." His tone had changed from the light, bantering one of a moment before. "Centrifugal Force was a dream of mine, too. I made it come true. I needed to do that. And I never gave up the music, not really. How could I?"

She studied his face for a moment, relieved at the ring of truth in what he said before she began again. "I guess I'll have to accept the fact that you've made another of your dreams come true by building your cabin in *my* mountains."

He chuckled. "It would make things a lot easier."

"Things can never be like they were, Kane." She made her voice level.

"What makes you think I want them to?"

"You don't? I mean . . . I thought . . ." She was stuttering again, confused by the stab of disappointment that pierced her at his words.

"There's no reason we can't be friends, though. Is there?"

What nonsense was this? Friends. It was what a man said to a woman when he was tired of her, what lovers always said to each other when desire was gone. "We can never be friends, Kane." She wouldn't tell that kind of lie.

"You can't be sure of that."

The pulse at her throat was aching now. How could she be "friends" with the only man who had ever stirred her so deeply? Who still stirred her, she admitted to herself. She rose and picked up the brown bag.

"Don't you want to be . . . friends?" The dark eyes were unreadable.

She couldn't let him get the best of her. "Why not?" she said with a brittle lightness. She wouldn't have to see him that often, after all. Perhaps it was better this way. "Well, I'd better go. I said I'd be back in an hour."

He tossed the basketball from one hand to the other. "Rachel?" he called when she reached the gate. She turned her head back over her shoulder. "I'll see you tomorrow. At the wedding, remember? Are you providing a band?" She nodded curtly. "Good. Then save me a dance. It's the least you can do for a . . . friend."

7

THE FRAGRANCE OF ORANGES drifted up to Rachel's appreciative nostrils. "Umm. Constant Comment." She kicked off her espadrilles and stretched her long legs out on the couch.

Catherine sat in Gran's ladder-back rocker, her spoon tinkling cheerfully against the sides of a porcelain cup. "You've done a wonderful job, Rachel Diane. It's going to be absolutely lovely. Avery would be proud."

"Avery Ellman . . ." Rachel hadn't thought of him in years. Avery of the rapier wit that never could mask his natural warmheartedness. He had designed parties for Catherine during the time before the accident, when Rachel had lived with her parents in Catherine's house. A soft smile curved Rachel's lips. "I used to think of him as some . . . wonderful magician. He would appear in a puff of smoke once or twice a year and transform my lonely . . ."

The tinkling spoon was still. "Your lonely life in that big old house of mine?" Catherine finished for her.

"I'm sorry." Rachel busied herself adding sugar to her tea. "That was thoughtless of me."

"Those years before you came here weren't happy ones for you." Catherine's voice carried no bitterness. It was merely a statement of fact.

"No, they weren't," Rachel admitted in a low voice.

Catherine leaned her head against the runged back-rest and closed her eyes. The faint creaking of the old rocker was a comforting sound.

"Catherine?"

"Yes?"

"I . . . I wanted to tell you. I'm glad you came."

"So am I." Catherine's lashes fluttered up. She stared musingly at the crammed-full bookcase that covered one wall. Gran belonged to several book clubs, and Rachel always teased her that no matter how many bookcases she had, they would always be overflowing.

"Every time I look at Ethel's books, I think of the library at my house. All those gold-tooled leather bindings. I ordered them in one huge lot the year before Phillip was born so they'd match." Catherine shook her head ruefully. "Of course, I had the pages cut and was sure they were all broken in properly. But some of them have never been read. The pages are dry. Brittle. Books need to be used, did you know that? The oil from human hands is necessary to keep them supple." Catherine took a sip of her tea. "I believe I'm rambling." She set the cup back in the saucer.

"I like it," Rachel encouraged. "I've never heard you ramble before."

"The last few years, those books . . . sometimes I think I'm like them. Dry. Brittle. Untouched by human hands." Catherine gave a small, nervous laugh, and the cup clinked against the saucer. Steadying it, she met Rachel's gaze evenly. "I have . . . kept something from you for almost twenty years, Rachel Diane. Something it was your right to know." Catherine's voice betrayed only the slightest tremor.

Looking away, Rachel came to her feet. The sinking feeling in her stomach warned her that this was probably a confession she didn't want to hear. "Maybe it would be better if—"

"Please sit down. This is difficult enough without you towering above me."

Rachel sat down. Catherine placed her empty cup on the coffee table between them.

"Your mother was killed instantly in the accident—"

"I know," said Rachel. "You don't have to—"

"Please let me finish," Catherine said curtly. She took a deep breath before beginning again. "Your mother died instantly. But Phillip...lived for several hours. They...they called me, and I went to him.

"He was...brutally maimed. Delirious. He rambled. Calling for Lydia. I sat very patiently by his side, the ever-dutiful mother. So proud of myself that I shed no tears. I shed no tears...." Catherine's voice broke. She waved a hand in front of her face as if to push away the pain. Then she went on.

"At the end, he became...lucid. He opened his eyes and looked directly at me. It was terrifying. The face was not my son, the face was... But the eyes. I knew the eyes.

"He asked for Lydia. I knew he was dying. I told him the truth. Then he asked for you. I said that you had sustained a concussion and several bad bruises, but that you were going to be fine.

"He was quiet for a moment. It seemed he smiled. Then he spoke again. 'Swear to me, Mother,' he said. His voice was very low. I had to bend over to hear him. 'Rachel goes to Ethel.' It shocked me so. I opened my mouth to protest, but he insisted again. 'Promise me. To Ethel.' There was no answer but one. I...gave him my word." Catherine leaned back in the rocker again. The opal-gray eyes were not dry now.

Inside Rachel, a dam was breaking. Emotions held in check for years roiled and churned against her own self-erected barriers. She had accepted the fact of her father's indifference, had come at last to nurture a fierce independence as protection against any man who might make her feel love, then refuse to return it.

"My father wanted me to grow up here..." Rachel breathed wonderingly. The very idea was a revelation. Her father's last thoughts had been of her, of what would become of her when he was gone.

"I was a proud, foolish old woman," Catherine said starkly. "I let you think it was inconvenient to keep you with me rather than admit my son did not want me to raise his daughter."

Rachel slid from the couch and knelt at her grandmother's feet. "I thought you... didn't want me."

Catherine gazed down at Rachel, making no effort to hide the wet trails of tears that ran down the fine, wrinkled cheeks. "I know. It took so long for me to understand that Phillip had made the best choice for you. That it would have been Lydia's wish, too. Here you had a chance for a fresh start. And I'm glad now your father was able to force that promise from me. I never would have given you up otherwise."

It was too much to absorb all at once. Rachel had to pull away. She half stumbled to her feet but had no idea what to do with herself next. She gestured toward the teapot.

"Do you want some more tea?"

"You can't forgive me, can you?"

"Oh, Catherine... that's not so...."

Catherine sighed resignedly. "Well, at least I've told you. Perhaps now I'll rest a little easier at night."

Rachel reached for the teapot. Her hands were steady as she filled both their cups.

"Sugar?"

"You know I never take sugar. A dab of milk will do. Where are the tissues?"

"On the windowsill. No. It's all right. I'll get them."

"What on earth are you staring at, Rachel Diane?"

"You."

"My powder is streaked, isn't it?"

"Did I ever tell you how much I love you?"

"Not since you were a very young child."

GRAN AND GIDEON WERE MARRIED the next day in the old schoolhouse. The ceremony itself was brief, with only the immediate family present. Gran shone with an inner light in the blue silk and linen shirtwaist dress that Catherine had bought for her. Gideon wore his only suit, of a rather unseasonable black wool with a string tie. The early-afternoon sun filtered in through the old-fashioned windows, bringing out the rich depth in the worn hardwood floor and winking like a portent of future happiness on the simple gold band that sealed their vows.

The next few hours flew by as Rachel supervised the final preparations for the party. Each boulder table had to have its own arrangement of wildflowers in enamelware bowls and teapots. The gingham-clothed tables in the schoolhouse had to be crowned with Kelly's creations of pine boughs and cones interwoven with tiny gold pans and miniature picks and shovels, here and there a nugget shining out.

Then it was six o'clock, and the first guests were arriving before Rachel had time to catch her breath. Leaving Carlos to man the punch table, Kelly to handle the food and Max to help the band set up, she went up to the house for a long drink of cool water and a few moments to herself.

Through the upstairs dormer window Rachel could see Catherine, lovely as a flower in her soft, rosy print dress with the peplum waist and ruffle-edged neck scarf, chatting companionably with Rachel's Aunt Jannie.

Jannie and her husband, Miles, had arrived just the day before from Seattle, where Miles was employed by a large trucking firm. In her mid-fifties now, Jannie resembled Gran more and more, at least physically. But in temperament she was more like her son, Chris—easygoing, without that need to "take things in hand" that was so much a part of Ethel Carver Gentry.

"Gentry." Rachel tasted the word. It would take some getting used to, thinking of Gran as married again. Still, the idea was not at all disagreeable.

Below her on the street, Mary Short approached Catherine and Jannie. Mary was holding a pie. Cherry, no doubt. Rachel giggled to herself, recalling Gran's frustration of the day before. People were arriving in groups of twos and threes, having parked their cars along the side of the road. After greeting the bride and groom, they carried their offerings in plastic containers and covered serving bowls into the schoolhouse, where Kelly would see they were set out temptingly as part of the buffet.

This was the moment Rachel loved most. When the guests were gathering and she could step back and know that through her art people would feel joy, have fun and perhaps come away with a sense of the quicksilver magic in life.

Jannie had gone into the schoolhouse with Mary Short. Catherine was waving at someone whom Rachel couldn't see at first because the trees blocked her view.

Rachel felt it would be Kane. And it was. She watched, swallowing the knot of unbidden tenderness that formed in her throat as he greeted Catherine warmly. He looked so dear and handsome in the creamy-chocolate jacket that clung to his broad shoulders. There were what appeared to be loaves of bread wrapped in foil tucked under his arm, and he carried a small jar with a bow tied around it in his free hand. Catherine took the jar from him and hooked her arm through his, leading him to the schoolhouse.

Rachel took a moment to run a brush through her free-flowing hair and spray an extra mist of Caleche on the pulse at her throat before descending to join the party.

Johnny met her on the lawn. "Cousin Rache, I'm all dressed up." His shiny little face beamed up at her proudly. "When do we get to eat?"

Rachel knelt and straightened the collar of his bright Western shirt. "I think you're the best-looking man here. Do you know that?"

"Aw, gee." Johnny looked mildly embarrassed. He stubbed at the grass with a miniature cowboy boot. "You look pretty good, too . . . for a girl. But when do we get to—"

"Eat?"

"Uh-huh."

"Well, I'm not sure all the food is here yet, but I'll bet you can have some punch. Just be sure to tell Carlos you're not twenty-one yet," Rachel teased.

"Why?"

"Because there are two kinds of punch. One for growing boys and one for—never mind." She took Johnny's hand. "Let's go inside together, and I'll make sure you get the right kind."

Since some of the guests were already helping themselves, spooning a variety of favorite recipes onto the tin
plates Rachel had provided to fit with the gold-rush
theme, Johnny went ahead and dished up. Rachel supervised fondly as he picked and chose from among the
offerings.

Kane was over at the punch table talking with Analise
Williams, who lived in the trailer park in Downieville.
Rachel had to admit that Analise looked wonderful. She
had changed her wispy blond hair to a more becoming
style—shorter, with more fullness around her face—and
her clinging persimmon-colored jersey dress showed off
her petite figure to perfection.

Kane waved casually at Rachel when she entered the
schoolhouse, but he couldn't seem to tear himself away
from his chattering companion long enough to come
over and say hello.

"This is all I want now," Johnny said from below her
elbow. His plate was piled so high it appeared as if it
might overflow. "I think I'll go sit on one of those tree
chairs." Grasping a handful of napkins and a knife and
fork in a fist that could barely hold so much, he took his
feast outside.

"In case you haven't noticed, there's a guy over there
who keeps looking this way." Kelly leaned across the
buffet table, her voice low, her hazel eyes flashing with
elfin mischief. "You do know which one I mean, don't
you?"

"I haven't the faintest idea." Rachel popped a cherry
tomato in her mouth and straightened a fan of forks.

"The blonde in the brown jacket. With the broad
shoulders and sexy dark eyes? Honestly, Boss. You have
to learn to be more observant."

"Your tongue's hanging out, Kell," Rachel remarked caustically.

"It's the twentieth century," Kelly parried. "Or hadn't you noticed? Women get to look, too, these days."

"Looking's one thing. Salivating's another."

Kelly sighed. "Unfortunately, I've had to come to grips with the fact that he's chosen you over me."

"And just what has brought you to that startling conclusion?" Rachel readjusted the ruffle of endive underneath a tomato aspic. Normally she didn't engage in silly banter with her employees, but she found herself unaccountably curious about what exactly Kelly had observed.

"Well, he's been buttering up Ethel, for one thing. And since she just got married, I've determined it's not her he's after."

"If I ever come to my senses and fire you," Rachel suggested dryly, "you might try opening up a detective agency."

Kelly's smug grin widened. "Taste this." She handed Rachel a slice off of a crusty loaf. The bread was spread with a thick red-brown jam. Rachel bit into it grudgingly. The taste was hearty yet somehow miraculously not heavy, just hinting of buckwheat, with the tartness of the jam a perfect complement.

"Did I add that he can cook?" Kelly was warming to her subject. "Your grandmother Ethel's recipe for seven-grain sourdough. He picked the gooseberries himself for the jam. Managed to squeeze out four small jars from the prickly little devils. That really impressed your grandmother, Ethel, who says she hasn't had gooseberry jam since—"

"It's very good. I think I'll go and see how the band is doing."

"Oh, Max can handle that. Did you know that gooseberries are pretty rare? I mean, you don't see a lot of them and—"

"If you don't stop right now," Rachel threatened, "I'm going to hit you over the head with this tomato aspic."

Kelly giggled. "Did I say something wrong?" She put on her best stage whisper. "Don't look now, but Mr. Wonderful is headed this way."

"Hello, friend." His grin dared her to rise to the bait.

"So glad you could come." Rachel focused on a spot over his shoulder, as if hoping someone more interesting would be arriving soon.

"I wouldn't have missed it for the world."

"I see you haven't wasted any time making new friends." Rachel waved a greeting to Analise, who was accepting a refill from a beaming Carlos.

"You look wonderful in green," he said with teasing irony. Before she could formulate an appropriately acid retort, he thrust a plate at her. "Aren't you hungry? I'm starved. Let's dish up and go outside."

"But I have to—"

"Try the tomato aspic." Kelly giggled, holding out a serving spoon. Rachel shot her a quelling look but accepted the spoon.

They found two free chairs on the side porch of the house. Rachel concentrated on her food, feeling curiously awkward. Down in the schoolyard the band had started playing.

"Your grandmother makes a beautiful bride," Kane said, gazing off with Rachel to where the gray-haired woman in the blue dress swayed in the arms of her new husband.

"I never thought she'd marry again," Rachel mused, more to herself than to Kane.

"Why is that?"

"My grandfather died before I was born, so she's accustomed to living alone. She always said she liked it."

"Maybe she did. But you can't fight love." The words had a teasing sincerity.

"But she's so independent."

"That doesn't have to change. I think Gideon loves her for who she is. There'll be plenty of . . . room for her to run her own life. Just wait and see."

Rachel turned to look at the man beside her. Several unruly strands of tawny hair lay across his brow. On reflex, she reached over and smoothed them back. "Don't you own a comb?" she chided, her voice indulgent.

He regarded her gravely, the threads of brown dancing in the blackness of his eyes. "I don't need one with you around." His voice had gone husky. Her question and his response were a part of their old litany, when they had been lovers, a part of the many phrases and special exchanges that had defined the nature of their belonging, each to the other.

Rachel hastily lowered her eyes to her plate.

"This is one mean chicken casserole," he said after a moment. "Do you want a bite?"

"I have my own, thanks."

"Not the chicken. You passed it up. It was a big mistake. Here. Taste." He held out a rather gooey-looking blob on the end of his fork, a dangerously endearing grin on his face.

She was going to refuse again, but he held it over her lap, and it seemed to be balanced rather precariously, the mass beginning to shift. If it fell in her lap, her silk chiffon dress would never be the same. Rachel opened her mouth. He popped it inside. The pointed tongs whispered across her lower lip as he withdrew the fork.

She chewed obediently. "Not exactly coq au vin."

"Ruth Daniels will be crushed."

Rachel wrinkled her nose and swallowed. "Not if you don't tell her."

"Have you been to the lodge on Sardine Lake? I haven't heard any complaints about the food up there." Rachel shot him a suspicious glance. "Yes, I'm asking you out to dinner," he confessed. "How about Tuesday? They serve a beautiful leg of lamb on Tuesday, from what your grandmother Ethel told me."

Tuesday. "Will you love me forever?" he used to ask.

"At least until Tuesday," had been her reply.

Rachel set her plate aside and dabbed at her lips with her napkin.

"Did I ruin your appetite?" His tone was bantering, but she knew he was waiting for an answer.

The shock of hair had fallen across his forehead again, giving him an infuriatingly boyish air. She should say no, of course. The ridiculous "friendship" he had proposed the day before would never satisfy her, but the prospect of anything more was perilous to contemplate.

"I don't ever know what to expect of you," she eyed him warily.

"Then at least we're even."

"One day you want to be friends, the next you ask me out to dinner. I feel like you're playing some game at my expense." She was careful to speak softly, so that none of the guests nearby could hear.

Kane set his plate down and stood up. "Come on. Let's walk over to the bridge and throw some rocks in the river." He held out his hand.

Against her better judgment, she took it. They went down the side path through the garden, past the rows of green beans and the sprawling squash vines and the wild roses that grew along the fence, to the street. At the bridge, he led her down the short trail to the riverbank.

The sand found its way into her open-toed shoes, and she sat down on a small boulder to shake it out. Kane knelt, picked up a flat gray slate rock and stood again to toss it out across the current. The fluid strength of the movement, the way his shoulder muscles gathered and released, even under the fabric of his jacket, caused that warming flutter down inside her. The rock skipped four times before sinking.

The band was playing "Greensleeves," the tune a little faint at this distance but still distinguishable. "One of Gran's favorites," she said to break the silence.

"Will you go to the Lakes with me Tuesday?" He repeated his invitation, coming to crouch beside her, lifting a hand to tug gently on the tie of her drawstring neckline. "We'll sit out on the pier and share a bottle of Lacrima Christi and watch the wind blow the boats around. Then we'll go up to the lodge and have our dinner and we'll…enjoy each other's company. We'll let the future take care of itself, and we'll forget the past."

"We can't forget the past, Kane," she reminded him, as one would speak to an uncomprehending child.

He wrapped the drawstring around his finger, his hand brushing against the silky, golden flesh at her collarbone. She caught her breath.

"Can we forget each other?" he muttered gruffly, pulling his finger from the wrapped string so that the gossamer fabric held a loose ringlet before slackening.

To avoid answering such a loaded question, she capitulated abruptly to the much safer dinner invitation. "Yes. All right. On Tuesday."

He tugged at the drawstring again. "You didn't answer my question."

"I said I'd have dinner with you."

The flash of cool amusement that lit his eyes told her he was considering probing further. Apparently he thought better of the idea and shook his head, composing his features into an expression of exaggerated relief. "I was never so nervous about asking for a date since high school."

"Come on," she teased. "Since I've known you, you've never had much trouble in that department."

"You didn't know me in high school." His mouth twisted wryly. "They used to call me Pizza-Face Walker. I had acne so bad I should have worn a bag over my head. And that wasn't all. I was six foot two from the time I was thirteen, and I weighed one hundred and twenty-five pounds. Believe me, I had a little trouble getting dates. Why do you think I developed the program that became Centrifugal Force? When Chris called me a self-made man, I wanted to laugh. He didn't know how right he was."

"I didn't realize it had been that bad," she lied, then amended carefully, "At least, I . . . didn't want to realize it."

"And that suited me fine back then," he confessed. "You were so . . . cool and poised." He ran a finger along the line of her cheekbone as if tracing some mystical perfection. "And I was pretty damn sure you'd never had a pimple in your life." The straying finger outlined the wings of each brow. "I wasn't about to fall all over myself explaining to you how relatively new it was to me that a woman like you would even give me the time of day."

"Vulnerability isn't a sin," she said primly. She wished she could call the words back as soon as she'd said them. Though true, they were much too close to the source of her own internal conflicts to be anything but hollow coming from her lips.

His hand dropped to his side. "Come on, Rachel. I felt enough at a disadvantage as it was, waiting tables for a living when you already owned your own business. Are you going to tell me you didn't realize that, either?"

Rachel smoothed the airy folds of her dress over her knees. The gesture was evasive. But her answer, when it came, was honest this time.

"No, I'm not going to tell you that."

"Good." He sounded relieved. Brushing off a rock next to hers, he sat down.

Grabbing a handful of pebbles, he tossed them into the river one at a time. "You see," he said when the small stones were gone, "on the one hand, I was so proud of you. You were developing that special talent for giving your clients exactly what they wanted, even if those same clients hadn't the faintest idea what they were after themselves.

"I'd drop by the site on the afternoon before a party, hoping to talk you into taking an hour off for lunch with me.

"You'd have the chef throwing a tantrum and the floral designer pitching a fit, and your equipment wouldn't have arrived on time. And there you'd be. Calm. Absolutely unruffled by any of it. Knowing precisely when to make demands—or to coax—or to just plain listen to a complaint and come to a compromise."

Rachel had no false modesty about her work; she was good, and she knew it. Still, Kane's praise warmed her. Before he had often been curt and impatient when the subject of her career had been broached. But now here he was, telling her at length that he'd felt pride at her success.

A car rumbled across the bridge overhead. Kane watched it as it travelled up the cut and disappeared around the bend at the top.

"And on the other hand?" she prodded, curious to know more. He gave her a puzzled half frown. "You said on the one hand, you were proud of me...."

The half frown faded. He stretched his feet out in front of him. "On the other hand, I was envious as hell. You were really on your way. And I was dragging myself out of bed in the morning after working the closing shift at the pizza parlor, confronted with another day of pounding the pavement, of trying to convince some uninterested agent-manager to give me five minutes of his time.

"The rest of my band had wised up and gone back to Lodi. I was forced to pitch myself solo. And it wasn't a hot year for a guy and his guitar. I remember one high-pressure type telling me flat out . . ." Kane's voice became harsh and nasal in imitation of the prospective agent who had turned him down. "'Okay, okay. So you write your own songs. What else is new? What you need is a gimmick, kid. Shave your head. Wear black leather. Get yourself a dancing bear. But for you, your songs and a guitar? Well. Throw in five cents, and it's all worth a nickel!'"

Kane grinned. "Can't you see me now? Bald. In a black calfskin jumpsuit. Putting my trained bear through his paces?"

Rachel found herself grinning back. "Hardly."

"Neither can I."

Her smile dimmed as she silently acknowledged how little support she'd given him back then. "You never did talk to me about what it was like." She was making excuses for herself, she knew. But at this moment it was very important that he understand how it had been for her. "I...sensed that things weren't going well, but when I'd ask you how an interview went—if you'd had any luck on your rounds that day—you'd always just give me a vague smile and change the subject."

"I was twenty-three. And much too proud for my own damn good. Mariette tried to tell me as much later, but I wouldn't listen."

Rachel blinked. Mariette. He had mentioned the woman's name so casually. Too casually, Rachel decided. She was instantly on her guard. "You discussed me with Mariette," she said flatly.

"Never directly," he replied, still infuriatingly calm. "But she knew things had gone wrong between you and me. It didn't take a genius to see that without my saying a word."

What was the matter with him, she wondered with disgust as she felt her anger flare. Did he actually expect her to sit here coolly discussing the woman with whom he'd betrayed her?

"What did you tell her?" she snapped, rising and glaring down at him.

He lifted his head, his hard gaze unwavering. "Nothing." The single word grated along her nerves. "And before you get started, let me remind you *again* that there's never been anything between Mariette and me but friendship and mutual respect. How many times do I have to say it before you get it through that stubborn head of yours?" With that disconcerting animal grace, he was on his feet, confronting her eye to eye.

Rachel's heart leaped alarmingly in her breast. She should never have left the party with him; he was still much more than she could handle. The realization washed over her that she had done it again, allowed the attraction he held for her to take precedence over everything, let herself forget all about Mariette, let him trick her into accepting his dinner invitation, gone along like a fool when he brought down her guard with his flattery, with his amusing anecdotes about dancing bears and bald singer-songwriters!

"It . . . it was a mistake . . ." she heard herself mutter distractedly.

"What?" he demanded, his face impassive.

"I shouldn't have come down here with you. I . . . can't go to the Lakes with you Tuesday. I don't know what possessed me to think that I—that we . . ."

"Could try again?" he finished for her. "You're right. We can't. Not as long as you hold on to that ridiculous conviction that Mariette and I were lovers." His voice was uncompromisingly firm; his eyes held her rooted to the spot. "Rachel. Mariette is in love with her husband. They've been married for over twenty years, and happily so, because they *work* at it. If you'd ever let yourself get to know either of them, you'd realize that what I'm saying is true. Mariette has neither the inclination nor the desire to waste her time chasing after cheap thrills with other men. It's just not in her."

His implacable mask of moments before had dropped. "For God's sake," he added with desperate sincerity, "their daughter is like a . . . kid sister to me!"

Rachel felt herself weakening, realizing not only the logic in his words but how very much she wanted to believe him.

"Oh, what's the use." His voice had gone flat. "You've put up a wall against me. And I'm ten kinds of a fool to think I'll ever get beyond it." He was already turning away.

She reached out and grabbed his arm. "Wait. Please." He didn't pull away, nor did he turn back to her.

"I...all right. I believe you...about Mariette," she got out brokenly, knowing a secret corner of her mind held out against him but having learned enough lately about her own shortcomings to give him the benefit of the doubt.

"You're right about me, Kane. I do put up walls. It's an old habit that goes way back." Her tone was strained, plaintive to her own ears. "Old habits are the hardest to break, I guess...." At a loss, she released his arm and stared miserably down at her feet, feeling she had made a mess of things, fully expecting him to walk away.

But he didn't walk away. Instead of moving in the opposite direction, his shoes were facing hers. One step. Two. His hands were on her shoulders, moving in a light caress to ride the curve at either side of her neck. Her breath caught in her throat as he tipped her chin up.

Beneath the tawny brows, his eyes were tender. "Someday you'll have to tell me how bad habits like that get started."

"Some things are—too painful to talk about," she confessed haltingly.

"For now I guess I'd settle for dinner. Tuesday?"

Rachel hesitated, aware that if she accepted, this time she wouldn't be able to tell herself that he'd tricked her.

She nodded. "Dinner. Tuesday."

Faintly she could hear the band from back the way they'd come. "'Smoke Gets In Your Eyes,'" she murmured, the haunting old standard reminding her that they'd been gone from the party longer than she'd intended. "We should go back."

His finger brushed across her lips, burned lightly and was gone. "Eventually you have to let out those painful things. Or they poison you from the inside." He gave her a heart-shaking smile. "You're right. We should get back. I want at least two glasses of that magical punch Carlos is so generous with. And then I want the dance you promised me."

His hand slid down her arm. Her fingers readily entwined with his. "I forgot to tell you. It's a beautiful setting you created for your grandmother and Gideon."

"You ain't seen nothing yet." She grinned mysteriously. "Wait until dark."

"What happens then?"

"You'll see."

Kane was at her side for the rest of the evening. When the last fading rays of the sun slid behind the western hills, Rachel managed to slip away long enough to whisper in Carlos's ear. He turned over his punch table duties to Kelly and disappeared through the rear door of the schoolhouse.

When she went back outside, Kane was waiting at the foot of the steps. "You still owe me another dance." He guided her toward the swirling couples beneath the dark globes of the paper lanterns.

"But you've already had your dance," she protested. "More than one, if I recall correctly."

Not bothering to reply, he pulled her into the circle of his arms and close against him. She surrendered to the dance, allowing his body to show her the way.

Up behind the house, near the flume, an old locust tree came alive. Rachel's lips parted in a smile of satisfaction as the tree glittered, shone with a hundred gleaming pinpricks of light. The light spread, claiming the railings and eaves of the house, winking like so many tiny eyes from the cherry tree by the porch.

All around her the dancing couples grew still, seeming to sigh in unison as the painted paper lanterns over their heads expanded with brightness. Gold panning miners and rushing rivers leaped out in glowing relief, floating visions suspended on the night.

"Do you like it?" Rachel asked softly.

Kane gave a low chuckle and pulled her closer. His warm lips grazed her cheekbone; then he loosened his hold as they swayed in time to the music once more.

8

"NOW REMEMBER, DEAR. The pump must be turned off when you leave. And be sure to let Sarah know so she can come and get Nat. I've left a list for you on the table so you won't—"

"Gran. We've been over this a hundred times."

"I know. I just want to be sure...."

"You're to have a fabulous time, and you're not to worry about a thing." Rachel wrapped Gran in a last hug and winked over her shoulder at Catherine. "Now you'd better get going before Gideon jumps out of that Winnebago and drags you bodily away."

As if on cue, Gideon leaned on the horn. "Coming!" Gran called, but could not resist one last look around the yard to be sure all was in order. Rachel smiled confidently, knowing every sign of the previous day's revels had been swept away. Her employees had made short work of cleaning up and were already headed back to L.A.

"I hate to desert you like this," Gran said as she climbed into the Winnebago next to Gideon.

"Nonsense," Rachel replied briskly, then grinned. "I'm looking forward to a little peace and quiet. You can send me a postcard from Idaho," she added, tugging on the door to see that the latch had caught securely.

Gideon shifted the vehicle into gear and backed toward the flat to turn around. Catherine and Rachel lingered arm in arm in the driveway until the Winnebago had disappeared around the turn to the bridge.

THE NEXT MORNING, bright and early, Catherine took her leave. Rachel hugged her as tightly as she had held Gran and promised to come to San Francisco for a visit as soon as she could get away again.

"See that you do, Rachel Diane." The misty light in the gray eyes belied the imperiousness of Catherine's command.

The house seemed suddenly so empty with everyone gone. Rachel busied herself washing the few dishes in the sink, thinking how lovely the wild rosebud from one of the wedding arrangements looked in the cobalt glass bottle that had been Lydia's. Like a promise on the windowsill, the petals wrapped loosely now, just beginning to open. She scrubbed out the sink and polished the faucet until it shone, humming snatches of long-forgotten tunes under her breath.

Beyond the wild rosebud, through the window, the morning sun peeked between the branches of flowering quince, spattering the side porch with warmth. Rachel chose a novel from Gran's overflowing bookcase and went outside to settle in a lounge chair. She opened the book and read the first page but found that her mind kept wandering back over the events of the past few days.

She could see Gran, dancing with Gideon beneath the lanterns in the school yard, the soft blue fabric of her dress lapping like water against the black of his suit. It seemed she heard the tinkling sound of Catherine's spoon against the sides of the porcelain cup before she had told Rachel the truth about her father.

And Kane. Winning the race on the Fourth of July. Standing in the doorway to his cabin, hands stuck in his pockets, a smile of welcome lighting up the strong planes of his face. And later that same night, the unreadable expression in the black eyes when he had refused to make love to her.

Rachel snapped the book shut and groaned in irritation. Tomorrow was Tuesday. And tomorrow night . . . Really, she must get the man off her mind. This was to be her private time, this day and the two weeks to follow. The prospect of one date with Kane shouldn't interfere with her solitude. Perhaps a few little projects would keep her errant thoughts in line. . . .

BY FIVE-THIRTY Tuesday afternoon, Rachel had taken all of Gran's books from the shelves, dusted them and put them back in even rows. She had weeded the flower beds in the front yard, digging up each tenacious dandelion with unrelenting determination. She had vacuumed and swept and mopped and broken more than one fingernail, so that she had been forced to cut them all shorter and coat them with a translucent bronze-tone polish.

Waiting for Kane to arrive, she gazed at them a little regretfully but decided they at least looked neat. Then she raised her eyes to study her reflection in the full-length mirror in Gran's room.

The open-backed cotton sundress showed golden expanses of her tanned skin, and the color, a butter yellow, set off the lights in her eyes. Little hoop earrings dangled from her lobes, only partially hidden by the curled mass of her hair, which she had pulled back from her face with high-placed combs.

She heard his knock, three light raps. Grabbing up the bolero jacket that matched the dress, Rachel went to answer.

He was leaning lazily against the jamb, grinning at her through the small glass panes that decorated the top half of the door. As she ushered him inside, he gave a low whistle. "It'll be hard to keep my mind on a leg of lamb with someone as delicious as you sitting across from me."

"Can't you do two things at once?" she asked with feigned innocence. It was a definite effort to keep from sinking into the liquid depths of his eyes. She handed him her jacket. "Would you mind?"

He shook his head, eyeing the golden-brown skin of her shoulders.

"I want your mind on the road," she teased, laughing as he held out a sleeve for her arm. "Now let me get a scarf and—"

"What for?"

"Kane Walker, you know what condition my hair will be in after an hour's ride in your Land Rover."

"We're not going in the Land Rover."

"But I thought—"

"Come on. I have something to show you." He led her out onto the porch and pointed to the street, where a 1956 Buick Roadmaster, royal-blue and white, shone in the afternoon sun.

"I told you I'd fix it up someday," he said proudly.

"And I told you you were out of your mind."

"Looks like we both knew what we were talking about." He tilted her chin up with the tip of a finger. "You ought to have had more faith in me. I may take a long time doing it, but I always accomplish my goals."

"Don't tell me I've underestimated you. What other surprises do you have in store?"

"If I told you they wouldn't be surprises, would they?'

"All the same, I'd like to be prepared." *And I don't feel prepared at all*, she finished silently. He was so temptingly close. If she weren't careful she would throw her arms around his neck and melt right into him—right here. On the front porch.

"Shall we go?" He stepped back and gestured toward the gleaming car.

Rachel flew down the steps and reached for the door handle. "Ever the independent woman," he said from behind her, slipping his hand around to grasp the latch before she could do it herself.

She rolled down the window when they topped the cut, loving the brisk, faintly piney scent of the mountain air. Above them Grizzly Peak, its craggy face rugged and ageless, caught the last of the sun and shone gray black against the cloudless sky.

"Chris tells me you hiked up there a few times when you were kids," Kane said, noticing the direction of her gaze. "He also says you slid down a hill of poison oak and yelled at him to leave you alone when he scrambled after you."

So he and Chris had been talking about her. Rachel remembered that day, how proud she had been to be able to keep her balance on the treacherous path behind her mountain-born cousin. And how foolish she had felt when she'd slipped from the trail and tumbled down through the shiny green and red leaves. "There was no reason for both of us to break out in a rash. Besides, I wasn't hurt." She glanced over at the man beside her. "Except for maybe my pride," she admitted softly.

"And your absolute determination to avoid needing help from anyone."

Rachel narrowed her eyes, ready to answer the challenge in his words. Was he trying to tell her there was something wrong with wanting to take care of herself?

He spoke again before she could organize her thoughts for a stinging retort. "It's an admirable quality, self-reliance. One of the things I've always liked best about you."

How was she supposed to put him in his place when he adroitly turned a criticism into a compliment? "Thanks," she said shortly, twisting her lips into a wry approximation of a smile. "But I seem to recall your saying once—"

"That your damn career was ruining us?" He shrugged, then added matter-of-factly, "You were twenty-two, only a year younger than I was. But you already owned Illusions Unlimited. I felt threatened, Rachel. I felt like a . . . momentary diversion—someone who could never hold a woman like you."

"You knew I was—" she hesitated, finding it difficult to say the words "—inexperienced when I met you. That must have told you something about the likelihood of my considering you a diversion."

He glanced at her, his gaze warm and direct before he turned his eyes back to the road. She looked down at her hands.

"I tried to convince myself of just that," she confessed, twisting her fingers, then forcing them to lie quiescent in her lap. "That you couldn't hold me. It's ironic that the one who wound up believing it was you."

His smile was gentle. "Hey, we said we wouldn't talk about the past. Tonight is . . . you and me and the magic of your mountains. As we are right now. Wounded and wiser, maybe, but still open to . . . enchantment."

Rachel was silent for a moment, pondering his choice of words. Enchantment. She created it for a living. Didn't she have a right to some herself? And if there was anyone who could weave a spell around her, it was this man.

No matter what had passed between them in the first tumultuous flowering of her womanhood.

She smiled a little tremulously, nodding her head. He caught the slight signal and shot her an answering grin.

Kane slowed the car when they passed Cannon Point and drove through Downieville at the posted speed limit. A few of the "boys on the bench," as the old-timers who sat in front of the Downieville Grocery were affectionately known, raised arms in salute as the car went by.

Just outside Sierra City, they got their first glimpse of the Sierra Buttes. Spectacular and uncompromising, the chain of gray cliffs towered over the surrounding hills, a trailing rim of thrusting sentinels varying in height, seeming to regard with a merciless patience the rolling, mesquite-covered sweep of the land below. They turned off the highway at Bassett's Station and made their winding way up to Gold Lake Road, past the point where the pavement gave out to rocky ground, over the small bridge to the cleared area where several campers and cars were already parked.

Out on the floating patio connected to the pier on Lower Sardine Lake, they opened the bottle of wine Kane had brought and chatted with the other guests who were waiting for the bell to ring announcing the eight o'clock meal.

The wind had picked up and was quite chilly, ruffling the gray-green surface of the lake and buffeting the orange sail of a small craft, heeling it over on its side till the lone sailor righted it at the last minute. The Buttes above were beautiful, different in shape from this side, indigo and magenta as dark approached.

Kane wrapped his red canvas jacket around Rachel. She leaned back with her head nestled in the curve of his shoulder to watch the burning purple of the setting sun.

The lapping of the water against the rocks was hollow, exhilarating and soothing at the same time.

"It's like a little pocket out of time," she mused, the wind carrying her low words back to him. "God's pocket. Full of precious stones, the lakes. And the towering patience of His love—that's the Buttes. And the blessing of His breath to give all life." She sighed. "Gran said that. The first time she brought me here. I was a very bitter little girl with a chip on my shoulder. But I'll never forget that first time I came here."

Kane's arms linked beneath her breasts. She felt the warm caress of his lips against the coiling, wind-tossed thickness of her hair.

When the dinner bell rang, they strolled up to the lodge beneath the sheltering roof of pine branches, shoes crunching on the carpet of pine needles, Kane's arm around her shoulders.

They shared a small table by a window; it had a view of the lake framed by two tall cedars. Out of habit Rachel noted the friendly efficiency of the service, but she knew the key element to her enjoyment was her dinner companion. The dining room was full. But to her there was only the two of them. The intimacy of their shared glances blocked out everything else until there was only his deep voice and her laughter, the clink of their glasses in a wordless toast, the warm clasp of his fingers when she rested a hand on the table and he covered it with his own.

"More coffee?" asked the smiling waitress. Rachel shook her head. Glancing around the cozy dining room, she realized she and Kane were the last to leave. The cook and hostess sat at a small counter in one corner, sipping steaming cups of their own, waiting good-naturedly for the one remaining couple to be on their way.

Kane squeezed her hand gently. "Ready to go?"

"I suppose we ought to," she agreed, wishing she could sit here forever, talking softly with Kane about nothing in particular, enjoying the smoky sound of his voice and the tranquillity that came after a satisfying meal.

The crisp night air was bracing, nipping tiny cold kisses against her cheeks so that she pulled the warm cocoon of his jacket tighter around her. They wandered down for a last look at the lake and stood close together, sharing the heat of their bodies. The moon was waning, but still its reflection broke and scattered across the wind-ruffled surface in an enchanting dance of random light. His hand snuggled against her nape, the fingers strong and steady through the layers of warming cloth.

"I think you've cast a spell on me," she murmured, leaning closer to him.

"But you're the one who weaves the spells," he countered, turning the collar of his jacket up to protect her exposed neck, then tugging her around to face him. "Your eyes are all gold right now."

"It must be the moon."

Her softly parted mouth beckoned, and he touched his lips to hers, nipping little kisses as the wind had done. But not cold. No, never cold. She thrust the tip of her tongue beyond his teasing lips and ran a flicking trail along the surface of his smooth white teeth. He bit gently but allowed her to enter fully, and she tasted the vulnerable inner softness of his mouth, feeling his hands slip beneath the jacket to pull her closer still. Then he took his mouth from hers and buried his face in the silky tangle of her hair.

"Come home with me. Just for tonight."

And what about tomorrow? Rachel knew she should ask. But the spell he had woven, soft as velvet, ensnared her as surely as the warm steel of his arms. "Yes." She only mouthed the word, but still she knew he heard. They turned together and headed for the car.

The humming of the tires when they reached paved road lulled, seduced her. She leaned her head back against the seat and allowed her lashes to cover her eyes. Just for a moment. . . .

The firm pillow that had wrapped itself around her shoulder moved. She nuzzled closer to it. It smelled of Kane. Of woods and promise and sweet fulfillment.

Rachel opened her eyes. He was smiling down at her, his arm the cradle in which she'd slept. The car was still. They must be at his house.

"I hated to wake you," he said. "You're trusting as a baby when you sleep. All soft. . . ." He tipped her head up with his free hand so she had to meet his eyes. "Do you still want to go inside?"

"That's an unfair question. I just woke up." She stretched and yawned, then turned to regard him gravely. "It would probably be unwise."

He reached for the key that was still in the ignition. She stopped him with a hand on his arm.

"But yes. Let's go inside."

"It's your last chance to change your mind." His voice was level. "I've waited a long time, Rachel. I can wait longer if you'll just say so before this goes any further."

"Where you acquired all these scruples I'll never know." She wrinkled her nose at him. "Can't you just sweep me off my feet and be done with it?"

"Don't think I haven't given the idea serious thought." He arched a gold eyebrow, considering. "But no. Last time I did that, you didn't speak to me for six years."

Her eyes slid away to peer through the windshield at the looming, dark shape of the cabin. Yes, he'd taken her hard and fast that night in her apartment, without a thought for all that stood between them. But hadn't she given as good as she'd got?

He captured her chin again and made her face him. "I'm sorry about that night. You can't know how I've"

"Shh." She pulled the gentle fingers up to her lips and kissed them, lightly, on each tip. "Let's go inside."

Kane built a fire, and they shared the last of the wine, sipping it slowly as they nestled among the bright pillows. The stark glory of the Buttes, captured in oil above the fireplace, was an echo of where they had been; it would take no artist's rendering, though, to show Rachel where she was going now. She watched fondly as he removed his shoes and socks, rolling the socks as he always did, tucking them into the shoes.

The flames licked around the logs, dancing brightly even as they consumed. He set his glass on the smooth stones and stretched out before her, fiddling with the clasp of her sling-back pump. She pointed her toe, and the strap slid down. He slipped the shoe from her foot, his palm a brushing caress along her arch. Tossing the pump aside, he went to work on the other, pausing only to slide his hand up the singing curve of her calf to that sensitive place behind her knee. Rachel gasped softly.

Kane took her half-full glass from her and set it next to his. She leaned back among the pillows, sighing deeply, watching the dancing flame shadows on the nubby beam-crossed ceiling.

"I've thought a lot about your ankles," said a voice from somewhere around the vicinity of her feet.

A bubbling laugh escaped her. "And what did you decide?"

"That the way they curve down into your heels is a minor miracle." She felt his devilish finger, tracing the curve he described. "And your calves..." The finger moved higher, then came around to the front of her outstretched leg. "And this glorious shinbone...and this knee..."

"That knee in particular?"

"One at a time." The naughty digit swept up her thigh, leaving a trail of goose bumps beneath the protective cloth of her dress. There was an open palm at her waist, now—grasping, pulling her length against him.

He lowered his mouth to nip at her shoulder, catching the strap of the sundress in a flash of gleaming, bared teeth and tugging it down. His hand replaced the strap, rubbing, massaging at the satin skin, moving lower to claim a waiting, upthrust breast, flicking a thumbnail at the nipple that surged to life beneath the yellow fabric.

"I want to see you. In the firelight. With nothing but your hair to hide you from me." Deft hands tugged free the high-placed combs.

She rolled away from him and came to her knees, her hair a tangled, cloudy mass around her golden face, knowing that the fire behind him held her clearly in its light. She lowered the other strap, reaching behind her to tug the short zipper at her waist downward. She stood up as smoothly as any dancer, and the dress collapsed in a butter-yellow puddle at her feet, followed a moment later by the gold hoops at her ears.

Rachel heard the sharp intake of his breath as she unclasped the front hook of her strapless bra, uncovering the milky, dark-tipped globes, swollen with longing, to his hungry gaze. Her thumbs peeled beneath the elastic waist of her lacy half-slip and the satin garment slid to the floor on top of the dress. It took a little longer to unhook her stockings, and she made the most of the action, knowing he had always loved the fact that she never wore panty hose, aware of his pleasure in the revealing look she granted of a firm inner thigh, flexed and tightened so that the wisp of nylon could slide down. At last there was only the pale triangle of her panties. There she hesitated, suddenly afraid.

Her eyes flew away from the waiting length of him below her and toward the window that fronted the deck. The night would not allow her to see beyond. Instead it was herself she glimpsed, a dark reflection, but damning. With the firelight catching on her round, full breasts. Silvery and golden, she was. Every inch revealed. Who was this strange and pagan vision—surely not herself!

But Kane was beside her then, reaching for her shoulders, gathering her close gently, but with an urgency that would not be denied.

He was kissing her, relighting the fires. How they burned her, leaping to new life beneath his strong firm hands. She was lost, lost....

Her own hands clutched at him, oblivious to the faraway chiding of her mind, tugging at his sweater, pulling it over his head, tangling in the furred mat on the hard-planed chest. Then grabbing him against her so she could feel her breasts crushed against the ungiving iron of his.

They would not be still, her hands, fumbling with the clasp of his belt, dragging it from the loops, making short work of his slacks, satiated for less than a split second once she had pushed his briefs away, too. The hard proof of his manhood thrust against the close-curling hair where her thighs joined. She reached to clasp him, her small, prosaic moan telling more than words could do of her desire.

Kane laughed, a triumphant sound, somewhere between a groan and a primitive snarl of ownership, and pulled her, tumbling, down among the pillows.

Rachel fell on top of him, setting her hands on either side of his tousled head, pushing herself a little away from him, taunting him with the need-hardened peaks of her breasts. He was quick to return the exquisite torment, palming the dark-rose nipples then rolling on top to lay his mouth against the swelling side of one, his tongue trailing inexorably up to the aching crest, swirling like a tiny, solid whirlpool around the aureole.

Raking hands, her own, were in his hair, dragging him down to claim the upthrust peak. At last he did, taking the bud between lightly clenched teeth, then drawing it farther inside, where the liquid dance of his tongue made her writhe and cry out with growing need. She wrapped her long legs around his hips, urging him to enter her.

"Not yet. Oh, Rachel. I want it to last forever." He grasped a handful of cascading hair and tugged—tenderly but without mercy—seemingly impervious to her whimper of loss as he came away from her to his knees.

She looked up at him from her soft, embracing bed of pillows, yearning and open for the final union.

Her eyes devoured him, unashamed. He was as silver and gold as she in the firelight. But rougher, cut from harder stuff. The muscles of his arms flexed powerfully in the flame glow from the hearth. The broad expanse of his chest thrust out as he took a deep and steadying breath. His sculptured face was a magnificent study in light and shadow. And his eyes, black as midnight, branded her as his.

"In this, there is no one but you and me. No ghosts, no past mistakes to haunt us. Tell me it's so, Rachel. Admit, at least, that this is real."

Her nerves were singing. Surely the roaring torrent of her blood was answer enough. She moaned and reached for him, lifting herself off the pillows until she clasped his steely arms and drew him back to her.

He filled her then, his own need too great to hold himself away until she confessed in words that he was the only man who could make her feel like this. The only man who terrified and gave her joy and left her helpless at his touch.

Joined, they moved together, spiraling upward, leaping like twin flames toward a sky as broad and high as any they had known. Then bursting and cascading down, in a thousand sparks, to earth.

As their mingled breaths slowed, Rachel held Kane to her, wanting only to memorize with touch and scent the whole of him, defenseless now as she was in the afterglow of love. This was a world apart, just as he had said. A magic world inhabited by two.

It was really very sad that tomorrow, in the harsh light of the morning sun, she might regret what had passed between them here.

9

THE BED WAS WIDE, the mattress firm. There were plenty of blankets, but it wasn't long before they didn't need covers as they made love again by the light of the small bedside lamp. If before there had been an edge of frantic need, now their shared caresses were slow and languid, the final plateau reached on a rolling, expanding wave of mutual and satisfying pleasure.

Afterward Kane tugged the crumpled quilt from the foot of the bed and wrapped it closely around them, making a warm cave in which they slept.

RACHEL WOKE TO THE FEELING that someone was watching her. One eye opened sleepily to meet two smoky quartz ones.

"Is it morning?"

"Technically, yes. But it won't be light for a while yet."

"Lately it seems like every time I wake up I find you staring at me," she grumbled, remembering the previous evening when she'd fallen asleep in the car.

"I'm trying to figure something out."

"You do that by spying on people while they're sleeping?"

Kane smiled down at her in indulgent good humor. "I forgot how grouchy you are in the morning."

Dragging herself up to a sitting position, Rachel hugged the quilt against her bare breasts. "I don't consider it morning until I see the sun— What are you trying to figure out?"

"How I'm going to get you to talk to me without scaring you away."

"About what?" She pulled the quilt closer.

"You—us. What you've been thinking for the past six years."

"That would require a lot of talking."

"Maybe that's what we need."

Rachel studied his face in the lamplight. He looked earnest, almost boyish in spite of the faint dark shadow of his morning beard. "I've had what I needed, thank you. And you...performed very well." It was a cruel dig, but she was hoping to put him off, feeling much too vulnerable after the night just past.

He obviously felt her comment didn't deserve a reply. The skin over his cheekbones tightened. Suddenly he didn't look boyish at all. She retreated by lowering her eyes. "Isn't what happened last night enough for now?" There was a loose thread on one of the quilt squares. She tugged at it and concentrated on the way the material raveled and puckered.

"Look at me, Rachel."

She brought her eyes up, tilting her chin defiantly, all too aware that the gentle, coaxing lover of the night before was gone; in his place was this hard-eyed inquisitor. "Well, isn't it?" she asked again.

"No."

He was sitting Indian fashion, gloriously naked and completely unconcerned about the fact. She reached out to touch him, struck again by how much she wanted him and realizing in one corner of her mind that the power of his body over hers was infinitely safer than whatever he might say next.

Kane caught her searching hand before it found him. His grip was almost punishing on the tender flesh of her wrist. "Don't try to distract me," he warned. "As important as last night was—it's only the beginning. I want much more from you than that. I only hope you've grown up enough to be able to give it."

The steely determination beneath the studiously cool voice frightened her. She jerked free and scrambled from the bed, dragging the quilt with her for protection against his searching eyes.

"Where do you think you're going?" The voice was all steel now.

"Downstairs. To get my clothes."

"Running away again."

The truth of the statement cut deeply. Rachel wanted to scream at him in denial. Instead, with as much cool dignity as she could muster, she wrapped the down-filled fabric snugly around her and tucked the corner beneath her arm.

"Certainly two consenting adults should be able to spend the night together without the necessity for maudlin revelations of deep inner feelings."

"That's quite a mouthful, Rachel. Do you say that to all your one-night stands?"

"I don't go in for one-night stands," she snapped. "You, of all people, should know that."

"Then spare me the two consenting adults speech." He waved a hand in front of his face, the gesture contemptuous. His teeth were clenched. The little muscle leaped in his jaw, a sure sign that he was losing patience.

"I guess you've delivered such speeches enough times yourself to have them memorized, anyway." Rachel knew she should stop goading him, but some perverse impulse drove her on.

"It always comes to this, doesn't it?" He was making an effort to keep his cool, but his lips were a thin white line.

"I'm sure I don't know what you're talking about."

"Don't turn away from me!"

"Honestly, Kane. This trumped-up concern is completely unnecessary. You got what you wanted. You proved once again that you can coax any woman into bed—even one who's already learned the hard way what you really are!"

"And just what am I, Rachel?" His tone was low, silky, the growl that a big cat gives before leaping from cover and pouncing on its quarry.

Rachel realized she had pushed him too far. Still she couldn't hold back her parting shot. "Tell me. Do you browbeat all your conquests on the morning after? Does it make you feel more of a man?"

He was off the bed and upon her before she had time to turn away, his powerful hands digging mercilessly into the satin skin of her shoulders.

"You'll take your physical pleasure with me, but I'm not good enough to share what's in your heart! Is that what you're trying to tell me? Is it, Rachel?" His eyes were opaque, his jaw clamped tight. "You should be more careful when you use a man for stud. He might just go animal on you and rip you apart!"

She struggled against his harsh grip, a wild thing caught in the ungiving net of his superior strength. The trailing quilt coiled around her ankles, snaring her even more securely from below.

"Let go of me!"

"You'll never give me anything but sex, will you? Will you, Rachel?" He was breathing hard now, the chiseled planes of his face twisted in a frightening mask of rage.

Rachel gasped, the muscles of her stomach clenching. His hands moved up to clasp her shoulders. "So smooth, so beautiful. Everything I want...and what I'll never have...." His hands dug into her flesh.

Rachel's eyes widened as she felt the pressure. She pushed at his chest, palms splayed.

Her squirming and startled expression must have gotten through to him. He released her, shoving her away with an anguished groan. Rachel landed on her backside on the floor.

Kane stood above her for a moment, searing rage and horror at his own actions warring clearly on his face. Then he turned and went to the pinewood bureau. Yanking open a drawer, he grabbed a pair of worn jeans and thrust his legs into them.

"Go ahead. Get your things. I'll drive you home."

His back was to her, but the corded muscles between his shoulder blades and the quick, furious tensing of his arm when he jerked the zipper closed reaffirmed that she had pushed him far past the point of control.

Rachel felt unaccountably relieved; she knew he would not pry into her secret thoughts now. Unconsciously she had always known that the way to evade Kane was to dig at his manhood. She managed to come awkwardly to her feet, conscious in some faraway part of her brain that her own anger had fled, leaving her weak and boneless.

Rachel dropped limply to the bed. On the stand nearby was a three-photo frame. The stern, rather tired-looking couple on the left must be his parents. And that round, beaming lady on the right, his Aunt Sandra? Mel and Mariette Sayer were in the middle, their daughter, Victoria, between them.

Why would he have a picture of Mariette and her husband near his bed if he had ever played the gigolo with her?

But the further proof that she had been wrong about Mariette was pushed aside by her sudden insight into Kane himself. And a deeper, more painful one concerning her own thoughtless cruelty.

Kane had never been able to bear feeling belittled, less than a man, with her. How many times had she used the knowledge of that fact to keep from getting too close to him—without ever admitting to herself what she was doing? Six years ago she had been too young, too threatened by the power Kane had over her. She hadn't seen that he fought demons of his own.

"Kane?"

He was tugging on a pair of socks. The soft, pleading note in her voice made him hesitate. But only briefly; then he was pulling a T-shirt over his head. Fully clothed except for shoes, he leaned back against the bureau and crossed his arms over his chest.

"You'd better get dressed. You don't want to spend any more time than necessary with a dangerous, promiscuous character like me."

"You're not—I know you're not!" she protested, unexpectedly vehement. "You're not either of those things." A small sob caught in her throat, and she had to look away. "I...I had no right even to hint that you were," she added huskily, reaching out a none-too-steady hand to turn off the lamp.

Outside the sky was paler in the east. The jays and pigeons had begun their morning chatter. Kane came away from the bureau and went to the window. He looked out, both hands jammed in his pockets.

"When I was sixteen, I almost killed a guy. With my bare hands. His name was Davy Morgan. The school bully. It's an old story: ninety-eight-pound weakling gets sick of being creamed.

"I...I don't know what got into me. He just...worked me over one time too many, I guess. I started to hit back. And what do you know? I...connected. I saw the fear in his eyes. But I didn't care. I just kept hitting him. It was like I was going to...kill everyone who'd ever laughed at me, or called me a creep, or made me the butt of some mean practical joke...."

Kane turned from the window to look at Rachel. The pain in his eyes was a tangible entity. "I swore after I came to my senses I'd never hurt any living thing again. But just a moment ago, I could have."

"No," she said firmly, "you couldn't."

She wanted to go to him then, to wrap her arms around the broad shoulders and tell him with her body the words that were so hard to find. But that was the coward's way. Instead she kept her distance and forced herself to speak again.

"Listen to me. I...I baited you. I knew that you'd fought long and hard to build your self-respect. I used that knowledge without admitting to myself what I was doing to avoid...sharing my feelings with you. It was a cruel and thoughtless thing to do. But I didn't know—not really—until now, how very cruel it was." Searching the boldly masculine features for understanding, Rachel couldn't tell what response she had stirred in him.

Kane regarded her in watchful stillness. Something flickered behind his eyes. Was it disgust at her manipulation of him? Pity that she would resort to such tactics to keep him at a distance?

Rachel winced inwardly. What had possessed her to confess her weakness to him out loud? Silhouetted in the dawn light, proud, unmoving, he seemed the very essence of the unforgiving male.

"Put your clothes on," he said at last. "I imagine we've had enough revelations for one morning—even if they weren't the ones I had in mind."

WHEN THEY REACHED GRAN'S, Nat ran out to meet them. Stepping out of the car, Rachel greeted the eager dog, scratching him behind the ear and allowing several sloppy, doggy kisses to be swiped all over her face.

Kane leaned across from his place at the wheel and spoke through the open passenger window. "I'll be at the Cliffs this afternoon. So I'd advise you to choose another spot if you don't want company." The challenge in the warning was unmistakable. He knew she considered the Cliffs her private place. "You should have put up a fence while you had the chance," he added, as if in answer to her thoughts.

"Would it have done any good?"

"No." He shook his head. "No good at all."

Once inside, Rachel drew herself a bath. The phone rang just as she'd settled gratefully into the steaming tub. She let it ring several times, but whoever was calling refused to give up. Dripping bubbles and water behind her, clutching a flowered towel much smaller than the luxurious bath sheets she used at home, Rachel stumbled from the tub and into the main room, where the insistent phone droned on.

"Hello," she growled into the mouthpiece.

"Rachel?" Rachel grunted. It was Elaine, her redoubtable assistant at Illusions Unlimited. "At last. I knew if I just let it ring, you'd pick up eventually."

"It's seven-thirty in the morning, Elaine."

"I called last night. No answer. Don't tell me I woke you?" Elaine gave a self-satisfied chuckle.

"I was trying to take a bath."

"The mountain air must be good for you. Awake already and not even noon yet." An early riser herself, Elaine always knew the surest time to get a hold of Rachel was early in the morning, when you could generally catch her, unconscious perhaps, but predictably in bed.

"What's up?" Rachel prodded, trying her best to wrap the skimpy towel around her dripping body and keep from dropping the phone at the same time.

"A big one. I wanted to check with you first before working up a proposal."

"Can I call you back in five minutes? Let me dry off and put on a robe."

"Five minutes. I'm at home," Elaine agreed crisply. There was a click at the other end of the line, and the dial tone buzzed in Rachel's ear.

Casting a rueful glance at the bathtub, Rachel dried herself quickly and pulled on her robe. Then she dialed Elaine's number.

"All right. Who is it?" Rachel asked briskly, picking up the conversation as if it had never been interrupted.

"Sayer. Mariette Sayer." Elaine's voice held an edge of excitement. "I told you it was big."

"Mariette Sayer," Rachel echoed numbly.

"You do know who I mean? Mel Sayer, of Mel Sayer Productions? That's her husband. Rachel, the woman is famous for her parties! And their connections . . . out of this world! We'll have the whole of Beverly Hills locked up if we get this account!"

Rachel clutched the phone more tightly. Elaine had come to work for her four years ago. Of course, the older woman didn't know that Rachel had once done some parties for Mariette—before Rachel's bitter personal experience with the woman, of course.

"Rachel. Are you there?"

"Yes, yes. I'm here. Did Mrs. Sayer call you herself?"

"No. She's been using the Feastmaster for years, and she's perfectly happy with them, from what I gathered."

"Then who . . . ?"

"Louie Laird."

"But Louie works as Terry Stoltz's private secretary. What connection does he have with Mariette Sayer?"

"Really, Rachel. You're up there in the sticks for two weeks, and you're completely out of touch. Louie was fed up with playing valet and body servant to that chintzy Terry Stoltz."

"Terry Stoltz is a good client," Rachel remarked defensively.

"Terry Stoltz is cheap," Elaine shot back. "Anyway, Louie's no longer with him. Louie Laird is now personal secretary to Mariette Sayer."

"But Louie hooked us up with Stoltz. Does that mean—"

"Of course not!" Elaine cut in, impatient as always. "I've already talked with his new assistant, and Stoltz has no intention of changing party coordinators."

"Well. Good."

"I swear, you'd think I didn't know my job," Elaine groused under her breath before returning to the subject at hand. "So forget Stoltz. Stoltz is solid with us. But if we play it right, we can have the Sayers, too. Listen—" Elaine lowered her voice as if trading international secrets "—Louie knows we're the best, and he knows it'll be good for him if we knock his new boss's socks off with a dynamite proposal for the wrap party of Mel Sayer's latest film."

"But if Mariette is satisfied with the Feastmaster..." Rachel hedged, playing for time. Perhaps she had been wrong about Mariette and Kane, but she still wasn't ready to resume a professional relationship with the woman.

Elaine let out a disgusted snort. "What kind of talk is that? I swear, has your brain gone soft? I call you about an inside track on a potential gold mine, and you imply that I shouldn't even bother to follow it up?"

"No, that's not what I meant...." Rachel dropped to the couch. The seconds ticked by as she tried to gather her wits.

"Rachel. Is something wrong?" Elaine's voice betrayed a growing perplexity.

"No, honestly. Nothing. To tell you the truth, I...had a late night. You're right," she finished with forced cheer, "my brain's gone soft from lack of sleep."

"I thought you were planning to get some rest this vacation," Elaine lectured tartly.

"I intend to. As soon as you let me off the phone." Rachel pinched the bridge of her nose between thumb and forefinger, ordering the tension there to relax. The only choice was to devise an effective stall. "Now. When is this wrap party and is there a theme?"

"That's more like it." Elaine sounded relieved. "The date's not set yet. Probably October. And it's vegetables."

"What?"

"Probably October. Vegetables—the film's about some starving people who stake out a public park for a vegetable garden. Very socially relevant and all that, but with humor. Wait'll you hear who's starring in it, and you won't believe who the director is—"

"I'm sure I'll be duly impressed." Rachel wasn't in the mood for a list of Hollywood who's who.

"Sorry." Elaine gave out her scratchy laugh. "Everybody's got a weakness. Mine's movie stars. Anyway, the Feastmaster hasn't even been contacted yet. Mrs. Sayer won't get a hold of them until she's more sure of the date. Louie figures we have four or five weeks before she gets around to it."

Rachel stifled a sigh of relief. "That's plenty of time. I'll be back on the thirtieth. That'll give us at least two weeks to—"

"Rachel. Louie said 'as soon as possible.'"

Rachel adopted her most authoritative voice. "Elaine. Do I know my business?"

"Well, of course, but—"

"No buts. I'm glad you called. It'll give me...something to think about. I'll jot down some notes and get some ideas in order. Then when I get back we can firm it all up."

"But what if—"

"Call Louie. Tell him what I said. If he thinks we've got to move faster, then call me back."

"But haven't we done vegetables before? I could look through the files...."

"Good idea. Get it all together. We'll add what you dig up with my new ideas, and we'll go from there. When I get back."

"Yes. All right. But if Louie says—"

"Worry about that after you talk to him. Just call me. We'll deal with it."

"We'll deal with it," Rachel repeated from between tight lips as she laid the phone back in its cradle. Loosening the sash of her robe with impatient fingers, she padded back to her bath.

The water was still deliciously hot. It worked its liquid magic on her tense muscles as she leaned back against the rim and closed her eyes.

Her mind, however, refused to relax with her body. She wasn't at all proud of the manipulative tactics she'd just used on Elaine. Her assistant was thorough, conscientious and highly motivated. Rachel had no doubt that she would put in hours of work to make the Sayer proposal an exciting one.

Rachel hauled herself to a sitting position and grabbed a washcloth. Working up a good lather, she soaped her arms and torso, scrubbing harder at her flesh than was strictly necessary, feeling totally disgusted with herself.

Her professionalism was central to her self-image. And it was unforgivably unprofessional to allow a respected colleague to waste precious time on a proposal that would never be submitted. Elaine was almost a partner. It wouldn't be acceptable to simply order her to forget the whole idea, yet explaining why would mean discussing matters so personal that Rachel hadn't even been able to go into them with Gran.

Sinking down so that the water covered her shoulders and the sweet-scented lather floated around her chin, Rachel groaned out loud. Circumstance itself had conspired against her. Louie Laird was ambitious, and his campaign to impress his new boss included Illusions Unlimited....

Her skin was puckering; the water had gone scummy and cold. Rachel climbed from the tub and toweled herself dry. Absently she reached for the bottle of lotion, slathering it liberally on her arms and legs.

The moist touch of her own hands reminded her seductively of the broader, rougher touch that had coaxed her to the heights of passion the night before. The lush color in her cheeks teased her from the still-steamy mirror over the sink. Rachel knew that look, though she hadn't recognized it in herself for over six years. It was the look of a woman well loved. Satisfied.

Only the mutinous tilt of her chin told the other side of the story. If she and Kane were to go on together, to go any further at all, she was going to have to talk. About herself—her feelings—which, in spite of the loving knowledge she had gained from Catherine, were still in a hopeless tangle. And she was going to have to find out for sure about his relationship with Mariette Sayer.

When the producer's wife had first announced her sponsorship of Centrifugal Force, there had been rumors. Rachel had taken the gossip as proof of Kane's betrayal. But hadn't she herself always discounted such tale telling as beneath acknowledgement? Wasn't the Hollywood grapevine notorious for manufacturing full-blown affairs out of innocent friendships?

Kane claimed the violet-eyed blonde was a friend and business partner. And no more. Why couldn't Rachel believe him? Had the two been lovers? Were they still? Or were her doubts merely an excuse to keep from committing herself to the man she had never been able to banish from her thoughts?

The photograph of Mariette and her family seemed to point toward his innocence. Was he, then, like a son to the producer and his wife? Did he think of their daughter as a kid sister?

Rachel closed her eyes, imagining how it would have been for her if she'd grown up as Victoria had, with both of her parents and a "big brother" like Kane.... But then she thought of Gran's twinkling eyes and Catherine's rosebud mouth and Chris and Sarah and little Johnny. Would she give them up to trade places with Victoria Sayer?

"Not on your life," she said pertly to her reflection in the bathroom mirror. "Besides, I would never be satisfied to think of Kane Walker as a big brother—never in a hundred years!"

Grabbing her robe off the hook behind the door, Rachel climbed the stairs to her room. Rest was what she needed after getting up before dawn.

AN HOUR LATER Rachel had counted the beams in the eaves above her head a good fifty times. Then she had tried connecting them with imaginary lines to form a myriad of geometrical permutations. Sleep would not come.

Rising, she went down the stairs again and scrambled an egg. The wild rose on the windowsill had opened during the night. Soon the petals would fold back and drop one by one. A short life, that of a rose. But in the glory of blooming, who considered the swiftness with which it would end?

"I do," Rachel confessed out loud. "That's me. Always worried about the petals dropping when the flower has barely opened up."

By two o'clock she knew where she was going. At least for the moment. Whether she was with Kane or without him, he filled her thoughts. Rachel put on her claret-red halter-top bikini. Tossing the matching wrap across her arm, she headed for the Cliffs.

When she reached the shadowed edge of the beach, she hung back. From beneath the fanning branches of a Douglas fir she watched the bronze play of light on his bare shoulders, hypnotized by the sculptured perfection of his back as he stood in the shallows, hands on his hips, staring off across the moving green water.

She slipped off her canvas shoes and went out into the light to join him, feeling the dry, gritty warmth of the sand between her bare toes. At the blanket that he had spread halfway between the water and the trees, she dropped her wrap and shoes. The small sound warned him. He turned.

The play of emotions across his features shot heat up her spine to meld with that of the sun on her bare skin.

"I wasn't sure you'd come," he said.

"What would you have done if I hadn't?"

"What matters is you did."

She took a few hesitant steps toward him. "I know we have to talk...."

"Later," he got out on a hoarse thread of sound. In three impatient strides he covered the distance between them. Clasping her shoulders with fingers that dug in just a little, he held her at arm's distance, devouring her with his eyes.

The grip on one shoulder loosened as his hand tracked a caressing trail upward to the tender indentation behind her ear. "We made love here once. So long ago. In that little clear space you showed me inside the clump of willows. Have you forgotten?" The questing fingers inched their way into the brown and cinnamon strands that curled against her neck. Rachel shook her head, wordless at the memory. "It's all I think of. Every time I come here," he murmured low.

"Do you want to...find out if it's still here?" she asked softly, conscious again of the web of desire, of how it spun and clung around them.

Kane tugged the strands of her hair toward him, pulling her along, until his muscled frame met her silken slimness in one long and searing brand.

"Woods witch," he grated into the face so close to his, before he moved to claim the waiting, parted lips. His mouth played on hers, improvising symphonies of taste and sensation. He took her lower lip between strong teeth and bit down hungrily, relenting at her gasp of mingled pain and pleasure, to run a gentling tongue along the lush curve.

Rachel responded in kind, digging demanding nails into the rippling bronze of his back, then following the scratching love strokes with the soothing echo of smooth fingertips.

"I made a mistake," he groaned, crushing her against him, melding their two bodies into one. "We'll never get much talking done here."

Rachel laughed, the low, throaty sound triumphant, as relentless as the river, mysterious as the shadows in haunted forest glens. "I told you this was my place. You should have believed me. Now you're in my power."

"What will you do with me?" he whispered on a passion-torn breath.

"Do you surrender?" She pulled away enough to meet his hooded eyes.

"That depends on the terms," he drawled, taking advantage of the distance to follow the swelling curve of one desire-heavy breast with a teasing hand that promised much.

"Terms . . ." She caught his hand and twined her fingers in it. "There are no terms. It must be unconditional. Complete."

"And if I refuse?" He raised her fingers to his lips, captured her thumb in his teeth and stroked it with his waiting tongue.

"It might be better if you did," she answered softly.

Kane released her hand. Rachel watched his eyes narrow in a puzzled frown. "Do you want me to refuse?" he asked evenly.

"Right now there's only one thing I want," she confessed with a ragged sigh, her touch straying back to trace the golden slash of his brows.

"Tell me." The voice was soft, but nonetheless it was a command.

"You're supposed to be surrendering to me," she chided huskily.

"Tell me what you want.'

"Tell me who's surrendering. That's all I want to know."

In a lightning move, he took her by the hips and hauled her against him. "Let's find out if that place inside the willows is still there. Then I'll show you who's surrendering. And you can tell me what you want."

Allowing her knees to buckle, Rachel caught him off guard and slithered from his grasp. On swift, sure feet, she ran to the stand of willows that grew out onto the beach. Pausing only long enough to see him bend and take up the blanket, she disappeared among the slender stalks.

10

THE SMALL, SECRET PLACE was still there, just large enough for Kane to spread the blanket. Rachel helped him, smoothing the sturdy cover over the tangle of stems and roots beneath.

"Now. Where were we?" he pondered when they lay together staring up at the cloudless sky. Swift fingers were undoing the neck bow of her halter top.

"Someone was surrendering," she cooed, shrugging her shoulder so that the loosened ties slid down the slope of her breasts. The small triangles of fabric fell away.

"And you were going to tell me what you want."

Rachel rolled over onto her stomach, knowing that the hardness of her nipples, when only his burning gaze touched them, spoke too clearly of her desire. Kane took advantage of her exposed back to undo the other tie in the center of her spine.

As swiftly as a mountain cat, Kane straddled her, his weight on his knees at either side of the smooth indentation of her waist. Knowing hands found her shoulders, massaging in a circular, rhythmic motion. Drawing in a languid breath, Rachel let it out on a sigh of release that turned into a moan.

"Cinnamon and silk," Kane grated, fingers brushing at the warm thick strands, lost within them for a moment before he smoothed them out of his way.

His tongue licked down her backbone, his hands not far behind. When he reached the barrier of claret fabric at her hips, he traced it with wetness, then followed the hot, moist touch with a focused, cooling breath.

Rachel quivered beneath him, burying her head in the curve of an elbow as he swept her last protection from her, sliding it down over rounded buttocks and clear of her tightened legs.

Then he was taking her by the waist, rolling her back to face the sky. He found the core of her womanhood with his eager mouth—stroking, laving—until she writhed and clutched the raw, honey head in supplicant's hands.

"Now. Please, Kane. Make it now . . ." she begged.

He lifted his head, lips swollen with the giving of pleasure, eyes hungry, aroused—almost dangerous in the male terrain of his face. "Tell me what you want."

Rachel squirmed beneath him until she had hold of the brief cover that shielded his manhood and dragged it off. Brown-gold eyes shot sparks at her small victory: he was naked at last, as vulnerable as she. With hands that would not be denied, she clasped him, giving in kind the rapturous torment, driving him near the edge of control with the sweet torture of demanding lips.

But he was the stronger. He hauled her up to claim her upstart mouth with his own, his tongue swirling, taunting, conquering hers.

"Now, wood witch. Tell me. What is it that you want?"

"Who . . . surrenders?" she got out, clutching him fast.

"By God . . . we both do," he groaned thickly.

She urged him with little mewing whimpers to claim her completely, but he held himself back until she gave him the answer he sought.

"Tell me, Rachel, or—"

"You!" she cried out, heedless of all but the roaring, tumbling river within her that only his absolute possession could contain. "You and only you! You're all that I've ever wanted. Then . . . now . . . and forever. . . ."

With a shuddering thrust he buried himself within her. A scream of pure ecstasy tore from her throat. The powerful, eddying current of desire carried them, swift and dangerous, toward the thundering edge of a waterfall and beyond, to drift through the spray and sheen of their falling, down into the shimmering pool of completion below.

Far overhead a hawk soared lazily, floating on the air currents in his perpetual search for unsuspecting prey. A willow wand swayed just in her line of vision. Rachel could see the black-spotted ladybug that climbed the stalk—slowly, patiently—to the very tip, then carefully over and back down.

Kane lifted his head from the damp comfort of her shoulder. With a tenderness that stilled her breath, he laid his rough cheek against hers. The butterfly wings of her lashes whispered near his ear.

"What do you see, woods witch?"

"A hawk. A ladybug. . . ."

Kane slid his weight to the side and gathered her into him so that their bodies still met in one long, moist embrace. Coming up on an elbow, he let his gaze sweep over her, from the tips of her bare toes to the tangled red-brown halo that lay around her face.

"This is how I remembered you. Always. Even when I was sure I would never hold you close to me again."

Rachel stretched languidly, aware of the tiny, dappling leaf shadows on warm flesh, the scent of pine and cedar, the hollow, constant sound, like a slow exhalation of breath that the river made not far away.

"It's a beautiful spot," he mused. "I can see why you chose it for your own."

Kane rolled over onto his back and lay there, one hand shading his eyes, staring up at the pale blue bowl of the sky. "Was it your mother's favorite, too?"

Rachel tensed. How had he known?

The lovely, sensuous mood evaporated, as insubstantial as a morning mist in the pitiless glare of the afternoon sun.

If Lydia could see her now... The thought made Rachel cringe.

"What . . . what do you know about her?"

"Certainly nothing you've told me. As a matter of fact, I don't even remember your ever mentioning her name."

"Lydia."

"What?"

"Her name was Lydia."

"I know."

The discarded halves of her suit had been pushed to the edge of the blanket. Could she reach for them without betraying by her action how suddenly naked she felt? Her hands longed to cross over her exposed breasts in that age-old feminine gesture of self-defense. She ordered them to remain still.

"What did Chris tell you?" she demanded flatly.

"Not a thing."

"Then who . . . ?"

"Your mother was born and raised here, Rachel. A lot of people remember her."

In her mind's eye, Rachel saw again the grizzled face in the Fourth of July crowd. "Lydia Carver," the old man had said, mistaking Rachel for the dead woman. Kane had been pumping the "boys on the bench" for information.

"What...do they remember?" It was an effort to keep the torn edge from her voice.

"That she was...'beautiful as sin.' And could care less about the fact. That even as a child she kept to herself. That she wore boots and men's clothes except when she worked at the Quartz, where they made her wear a skirt. That her eyes were green as a mountainside of pines from far away."

Kane reached for his swim trunks and tugged them on. Rachel grabbed her bikini, grateful for the small protection it offered. It showed no weakness to cover herself now that he had done the same.

"It took everyone by surprise when the rich lawyer from San Francisco swept her off her feet. I guess they all thought she wasn't the type."

"What type is that?" she asked sarcastically.

Kane shrugged. "You tell me."

They were both standing now. Kane gestured for Rachel to step off the blanket. She moved aside, feeling unaccountably weary. Grasping the edges in either hand, he was shaking the blanket out and folding it neatly.

"She's dead, Kane. There's nothing to tell." Rachel mouthed the lie without conviction, knowing he wouldn't believe it.

"That's where you're wrong." He tucked the blanket under an arm. "There's everything to tell. And I have a sneaking suspicion it starts with your mother."

Why did he have to keep digging at her? Yes, she had agreed to talk, to begin breaking down the barriers that lay between them. But not about this. Couldn't he sense how hard she had fought to escape from behind the shadow of the woman who had given her life?

"Give us a chance, Rachel," he said, his eyes searching her face. "You might be surprised how little power the past can have over you if you can let it go."

The adult Rachel recognized the truth in what Kane said. But the frightened child still cowered within, clutching the mask she had always hidden behind, the mask of pride and self-control.

"A chance for what?" she asked, choosing to ignore the dangerous whole of what he said and focusing instead on only a part.

"A future together," he replied blankly.

"What makes you think I want that?" she countered automatically. But her heart contracted. A future with this man was exactly what she wanted.

Kane's eyes went flat black. With a muttered oath he turned on his heel and plowed through the clutching willow stems, leaving her alone in the tiny clearing, her pride and self-control intact—her heart, an aching void.

It was several minutes before she followed, sure that she would find the beach deserted. But he was there, stretched out on the sand face up, his hands a cradle behind the tawny head.

When her shadow fell across him, he looked up at her warily. "How far do I have to go, Rachel? What do I have to do to make you trust me?"

She sank down beside him, gathering her knees up under her chin. The sand was hot from the sun. She sifted it between wriggling toes, wondering how he could lie there with the burning grains against his bare back.

"She didn't love me." The confession was like the sand. Dry. Burning. "I was a . . . mistake. She married my father because he found out she was pregnant and wouldn't leave her alone until she became his wife."

"Are you saying he married her because he felt he had to?"

"It was . . . I don't think he ever wanted any other woman after he found her. But I wouldn't call it love.

Love was... something I never thought of in connection with either of them. They had to have each other... couldn't escape each other. But it was a war. I was the by-product of one of their early battles." Rachel attempted a laugh at the aptness of her analogy. It came out a strangled sob.

"Your father... do you believe *he* loved you?"

"I didn't used to. But I know now he... thought of me the day he died." She took up a handful of sand and watched it trickle between her fingers. "At least he thought of me." She tipped her head and looked at Kane. "That's something, isn't it?"

In one of the catlike moves so familiar to her, Kane was on his knees and taking her chin between warm palms.

"Some people don't know how to show what's inside. They hurt the ones they love the most. With silence. And they don't even realize what they're doing." He was holding her eyes so steadily, as if he could communicate to her by the tender force of his gaze alone. A single salty drop escaped the dam of her lower lid and slipped down her cheek.

"Woods witch," he breathed, "you don't have to hide behind your spells."

"A little magic never hurts," she managed on a quavering sigh, brushing at her moist eyes before more revealing tears could overflow them. "Would you... think I was running away if I went in the water?"

She feared by the way he looked at her for a split second that he was intent on pressing further. But then he grinned. "Not if you let me beat you to the other side."

Kane was on his feet and racing down the bank before she had time to call him a cheater.

When she pulled herself up from the current on the other side, he was laughing down at her, dripping gleaming rivulets of water into a little pool at his feet. He reached to help her up. She grasped firmly and tugged, congratulating herself on catching him off balance for once. He toppled back in.

"That'll teach you to mess with a woods witch." She giggled before he stuck out a hand and dunked her beneath the moving surface of bright water.

FOR THE NEXT SEVERAL DAYS they were constantly together. It was a shining, golden expanse of time spent taking long hikes up winding deer trails to the various mines that dotted the hills.

They made brief trips into Downieville, where they had dinner at the Forks restaurant, lingering late on the patio there to pick out the constellations in the star-thick mountain night. Twice they caught the feature at the small movie theatre. It didn't matter if the film was one they'd both already seen. It was enough to hold hands like first-time lovers in the darkened space and share a bag of fresh-popped corn, their laughter mingling at the funny parts, exchanging knowing looks when the hero finally got the girl.

If occasionally Rachel thought of her well-ordered single life in L.A. to which she must soon return, a smile from Kane or the touch of his hands on her willing body was enough to dispel her uncertainties for the moment. He seemed content not to press her for more details about her childhood, or for the secrets in her heart during the six years they had gone their separate ways.

But late at night, lying in his bed in the languorous glow that came after lovemaking, Rachel wondered if his fleeting reference to their future together had been just that, something he had allowed to enter his mind—as a possibility because he still desired her—and then as quickly rejected when he had time to consider the reality more carefully. He'd paid a high price once before when he'd given her his heart. Maybe he considered it a fool's game to try again.

Besides, she reminded herself, women, as always, seemed to throw themselves at him. And now Kane had more than his charm and taut, masculine body to recommend him. He had a successful, growing business of his own. Rachel wrinkled her nose, recalling the warm, glowing smile Analise Williams had bestowed upon him while they'd waited in the line to buy their tickets at the movie theatre.

And the redhead from the Fireman's Ball, Leslie Farr, who had turned out to be a vacationing phys. ed. teacher from Nebraska. Kane and Rachel had run into her at the Forks just the night before. Poor Leslie. She was devastated to realize that her vacation was almost over and she and Kane had somehow never got around to that long talk about his special ten-point physical conditioning program. Kane had taken her address and promised to send her a brochure.

Rachel sighed. The tawny head that rested on her breasts burrowed deeper. Really, what was the matter with her? She was scared to death that Kane would ask her for a commitment yet as green as grass if any other woman so much as looked at him; worried that he hadn't mentioned again their future together and afraid to let herself think they might have one.

In the night-shadowed room, Rachel's lips curved into the faintest of smiles. She loved him, this man who lay against her now, loved him with all the depth and passion and merciless tenderness that her hungry heart could hold. Six years of denial had done nothing to alter that fact. It was inescapable. Like Lydia before her, she was powerless in the face of her own needful heart.

Yes, she could admit it now. It had been a kind of loving between her parents. But for Rachel and Kane it would not end in tragedy. They could build a life with plenty of space for each of them in it, as Kane had said of Gran and Gideon. If only he still wanted to....

Her fingers combed absently at the shock of hair across his brow. Kane stirred again.

"Go back to sleep," she whispered, pulling him closer, shifting a little until she felt him settle with his ear against her heart.

"Can feel you thinking," he mumbled. "It's keeping me awake...."

Rachel closed her eyes and drifted at last into a fitful sleep.

Her troubled thoughts conjured up anxious dreams, dreams that centered on a frustrating effort to get back into her L.A. apartment. Somehow she had locked herself out, wearing only a threadbare terry-cloth robe. Her first thought was the manager. But when she went to him for help, he claimed she didn't live there. Then she tried her next-door neighbor, but the neighbor turned out to be someone Rachel had never seen before. Next she went to her office, hoping to enlist Elaine's aid. But Elaine refused. Elaine was resigning, it seemed. Elaine thought it terribly unprofessional that Rachel had come to work in her bathrobe. Rachel looked down at herself. She was, indeed, still in her robe. The phone rang. In her dream Rachel answered it, but the ringing didn't stop.

Coming groggily to the edge of consciousness, Rachel felt around for the nightstand beside her and encountered a warm body: Kane's. Almost awake now, she realized she was in his bed; it was his phone that had roused her.

He stirred and reached for the receiver.

"Yeah . . . Hullo," he mumbled into the mouthpiece.

Faintly Rachel heard the voice from the other end of the line—unmistakably feminine. Kane switched on the lamp and propped himself up against the pine headboard, looking rumpled and appealingly bleary. Rolling over, Rachel inched her feet toward her side of the bed to rise, but Kane slid his free arm around her, pulling her back, settling her head cozily against him.

"Lord, Vicky. What is it?" The words vibrated deeply under Rachel's ear.

Vicky. Mariette's daughter. She tipped her chin up to give Kane a worried glance; late-night calls too often meant bad news. Intuiting her thoughts, Kane responded with a slight negative shake of his head, then pulled her back down against him.

His tone took on a grumbling edge when he spoke again. "Have you got any idea what time it is?"

But the lateness of the hour didn't seem to concern Vicky. She was off on some sort of tirade.

Kane cut her off. "Will you slow down . . . Vicky . . . ?" More crackles from the phone.

"That's none of your business." He snapped in response to something the girl had said. Vicky evidently changed the subject; his voice softened. "Look, little one. I know how you feel. But there's nothing I can do. They want what's best for you."

Vicky must have protested, because Kane became insistent. "They're your parents, and they love you. Try to give their point of view a chance."

Rachel began to feel as if she were a captive audience to one side of an exchange that should have been private. She tried to pull away again. This time Kane made no effort to hold her.

"No, I won't come back early," he went on. "And I wish you'd understand that I really have no right to get involved."

Kane's shirt lay over a chair near the pinewood bureau. Rachel slipped her bare arms through the sleeves and escaped down the stairs.

Once in the kitchen, she flipped on the light. The room leaped into cheerful brightness. The floor was chilly under her feet. She wrapped her arms around herself, wishing she had taken time to put on at least a pair of socks. Though she couldn't make out the words, she could still hear Kane's voice from above, the tone alternately tender and exasperated.

Well, she decided, standing here shivering would accomplish nothing. And something hot to drink would warm her up. She put the kettle on and pulled open a cupboard. A mind-boggling selection of herbal teas confronted her when she looked inside. Rachel stared at them in confusion as a wave of irritation swept over her.

It was one o'clock in the morning, and her lover was talking on the phone with Mariette's daughter. The shirt she had tugged on to cover her nakedness left her legs bare and goose bumped. All she wanted was a nice, hot cup of tea. Leave it to Kane to provide so much variety that even deciding what kind became a challenge.

With an impatient sigh she began reading the labels: raspberry leaf, golden seal, valerian, dandelion, skullcap, yellow dock.... Rachel wrinkled her nose. The man was either a witch or an herbalist.

Still, the names did have a familiar ring. Gran believed in herbal remedies, and Lydia had known them all. That one magic summer when she was eight, Rachel had come down with the measles. Lydia had plied her with chamomile tea and bathed her sore eyes with a soothing mixture of golden seal and boric acid. Rachel had recovered in two weeks.

The kettle emitted a high-pitched scream. Startled by the sudden eerie intensity of the sound, Rachel grabbed the first box that came to hand, plain peppermint. She spooned it into a tea ball and dumped the boiling water on top of it in the pot she found on another shelf.

She was just pouring herself a cup when Kane appeared at the top of the stairs. He had put on his pants, but his feet and chest were bare.

"What's that I smell?"

"Tea. Peppermint." She rose and brought another cup to the table.

Kane pulled back a chair and sank into it. "Sorry about that. Vicky's going through a major crisis."

"Does it look like she'll survive?" Rachel asked with false brightness, passing him the empty cup, which he filled from the pot.

"Only if she gets her way." He winked at her. "Hot stuff," he said, blowing on the steaming cup.

If she gets her way about what, she wanted to ask, but kept silent. From the little Rachel had heard, it sounded like a parent-child conflict and Kane was somehow stuck in the middle. The whole thing made her uneasy, though as yet she refused to consider why. She decided that if he wanted to talk about it, he would.

Apparently, he didn't. His eyes were focused on the top button of her—or rather, his—shirt. "I'm jealous," he said, one side of his mouth turning up.

Rachel studied the tea leaves in the bottom of her cup. *He* was jealous? What did he have to be jealous about?

"Of what?" she asked, nervously fastening the button he kept staring at.

"My own shirt," he answered with husky promptness. "It's wrapped around all my favorite parts of you—except for your head and your neck and your hands and your legs and your feet, of course. Those are also my favorite parts."

A chuckle escaped her lips before she could call it back. He was really too appealing, his hair more a tangled thatch than usual, his eyes heavy-lidded and lazily inviting.

He reached across the distance between them to wrap strong fingers around her wrist, tugging her out of her own chair and into his lap.

"Peppermint's nice, but you smell even better," he drawled, nuzzling her neck.

"You don't know what you're talking about." She brought her hand flat against his chest to push him away but found her fingers curling into the furry mat there.

"Because I'll take you over peppermint tea?" His own fingers were at work undoing the button she had just hooked.

"Peppermint has a lot to recommend it." She gave his hand a playful nudge, but he was determined. The button slipped free.

"Like what?"

"Well, it's one of the most trusted home cure-alls," she intoned in a feeble attempt to distract him from his seductive purpose. "Its healing properties are legend. It's . . ." Her mind went momentarily blank as his warm hand found her breast. "Umm. Excellent for chills, colic, fevers, dizziness. . . ."

"Dizziness?" he murmured, his hand creating just that sensation in her.

"And whatever else ails you," she concluded weakly.

Kane kicked back his chair and rose, holding her easily against his chest. "Not only do you smell good, you're an expert on herbs," he mused as he carried her toward the stairs.

"Not really. Lydia was the expert. I guess a few things she taught me kind of stuck."

He paused with a foot on the second step and looked into her eyes. "She must have been a fascinating woman," he said softly. "Almost as fascinating as her daughter." Instead of continuing upward, he remained poised on the step, as if waiting for her to comment.

"I must be getting heavy," she reminded him when the silence became uncomfortable.

After all, she reasoned defensively, it was past one in the morning. Hardly the time to dig more deeply into the hurts of the distant past.

He considered her remark, hefting her once as if testing her weight. "What you are is evasive. But heavy? I think I can manage to carry you as far as my bed." His smile was edged with gentle irony.

Tightening his grip, he settled her more closely against the solid wall of his chest and resumed his ascent.

11

WITHIN THE FERNY LEAVES, green and tender, the delicate asparagus spears were too tempting to resist. Rachel gathered them with care. There weren't many, but she could steam them tonight, and Kane would love them. Choosing a pair of ripe tomatoes, a head of red-leaf lettuce and some lovely, golden summer squash, Rachel carried her bounty back to the house.

Upstairs the begonia needed water, as did the philodendron. Tomorrow she would mow the lawn.

Rachel performed the few chores quickly, humming as she worked, anxious to be on her way. Today she and Kane had planned a hike to a pair of gold mines up behind the County Works, the Dig More and the Dig Less. Rachel grinned at the names. Had the Dig More been a richer mine? Or had the Dig Less produced more with less effort?

Over the sink, the wild rose had lost its petals. Rachel scooped them into the palm of her hand. First lowering her nose for a hint of the scent, she tossed them in the trash along with the thorny stem. The little cobalt glass bottle looked so empty.

Tomorrow—tomorrow she would find another rose.

Outside, Nat gamboled around her feet, begging not to be left behind. He wouldn't fit on the floor of the Mercedes, and she cringed at the thought of his careless doggy paws scratching the leather upholstery. But when he danced on his hind legs and gave her several eager yelps, she relented and found an old blanket in the garage to cover the seat.

"Now sit. Stay," she ordered firmly. Nat yipped happily and sat up very straight beside her, ears back, nose thrust out intently.

The plum trees on the Goodyears Creek Road were laden with fruit. Perhaps she and Kane would find the time to pick some. There was nothing like plum jam.

To her left, growing in a prickly tangle down to the creek, were blackberry bushes. Rachel noted with interest that the deep purple berries were also coming ripe. Now blackberry jam . . . that was her all-time favorite!

Feeling like a child and giggling under her breath, Rachel pulled to the side of the road and found a shoe box in the trunk. Twenty minutes later she had a network of scratches along her arms, telltale purple stains all over her fingers and a shoe box full of berries. Setting the box gently in the back seat beside the bag of vegetables, Rachel climbed in behind the wheel again and made her way past the County Works, across the small bridge and up the winding dirt road to Kane's.

A metallic blue MG was parked in Rachel's usual space beside the Land Rover. Kane hadn't told her he was expecting visitors.

Rachel slid in on the far side of the sporty little car and got out of her Mercedes. The license plate said Bob Sanders Foreign Auto. Rachel knew that name, a Beverly Hills dealership.

The door to the cabin opened behind her. Rachel whirled around. "I . . . I stopped to pick some blackberries." She felt a little silly, caught in the act of reading a license plate for clues to the identity of his guest.

"I can tell." Kane smiled at her scratched arms and stained hands, but the smile didn't quite reach his eyes. There was an odd, distracted look about him.

Rachel opened the passenger door of the Mercedes. Nat jumped to the ground and bounced over to Kane. "I just couldn't leave him behind. He looked so lonely."

"That's fine. Fine."

Reaching behind the seat, Rachel took up the bag and shoe box. "Here. Let me help you with those." Why did he sound so distant, so formal?

"I've got two arms," she informed him, grinning.

His answering smile was forced. "Come inside. This isn't exactly how I planned it, but there's someone I . . . want you to meet."

Rachel took a deep breath, squared her shoulders and followed him into the house.

The girl was sitting by the fireplace, Kane's guitar across her knees. Black hair, thick and straight and parted down the middle, flowed over her slender shoulders and down her back like a midnight waterfall. Her face was heart shaped with well-defined cheekbones and a slightly pointed chin. The eyes were as Rachel knew they would be, large and round and of the same melting shade of violet as Mariette's.

"Hello, Miss Davis." The rich, husky voice from one so young was rather startling. Smiling distantly, the girl turned her attention back to the guitar, picking out a few chords with knowing hands.

"Rachel—" Kane cleared his throat "—this is—"

"Victoria, isn't it?" Rachel tried to make her smile a warm one. "I think we met once or twice at your mother's."

One beautiful tapering hand lifted off the strings to tuck a strand of midnight hair behind an ear. Dangling earrings shaped like miniature chimes tinkled delicately with the action. "I'm surprised you recognized me."

"Why is that?" Rachel crossed to the table and set the box and bag on it. Behind her, Victoria began to play again. It was a ballad. Rachel's throat constricted. She knew the song, something about lost love.

"Well, you haven't done a party for Mother in years. And I was a lot younger then."

"You've grown up," Rachel said, turning again to meet the violet eyes.

"I certainly have." Victoria cast a teasing glance at Kane. "Some people are afraid to admit it, though." She set the guitar against the stones and came to her feet.

Rachel was struck by how tiny she was. Only an inch or so over five feet, looking delicate and very feminine in the high Italian heels and short, softly flared skirt.

"Have you had lunch?" Victoria asked, for all the world as if she were the hostess and Rachel an uninvited guest. "Kane and I were just going to throw something together."

"Oh, really?" Rachel let her gaze slide to Kane. He looked away with a nervous shrug and ran a hand through his hair.

"You'll have to forgive him," Victoria said, slipping a proprietary arm through Kane's. "He wasn't exactly expecting me." She looked up at Kane adoringly. "But after we talked on the phone last night, I just had to come. It was a spur-of-the-moment idea." The girl let out an airy sigh. "I drove all night."

"Your mother will be worried sick," Kane scolded, granting the heart-shaped upturned face a patronizing frown.

"I'm an adult, Kane. I have to make my own decisions."

"You're seventeen years old."

"I'm old enough to know what I want." The tapering fingers squeezed possessively on a corded forearm.

"You're going to call Mariette now and tell her you're with me."

Feeling very much the intruder, Rachel went to the sink and attempted to wash the berry stains from her hands. There was a lump in her throat. She swallowed and reminded herself not to overreact. It was ridiculous to let this seventeen-year-old girl intimidate her. Still, Rachel felt like an awkward, unkempt Amazon in her baggy old jeans and hiking boots.

"You can use the extension upstairs," Kane said. "Go on. Call her."

"Then will you bring in my suitcases?" It was a wheedling voice now, for all its sultry depths, the voice of a child accustomed to getting her way.

Rachel reached for a towel. Out of the corner of her eye she watched Kane tilt the pointed chin up higher still.

"Yes, little one, then we'll bring in your suitcases."

The intimate smile he got in response was not childish at all.

High heels clicked on the stairs. Rachel yanked open a cupboard and found a colander. Behind her, she heard the soft pad of moccasin-clad feet. Two hard arms encircled her waist. Rachel stiffened.

"Would you hand me the shoe box? The berries need washing."

"I had no idea she'd pull something like this. I hope you understand...."

Rachel lifted her shoulders in a studiedly casual shrug. She was beginning to understand all too well.

"She's just a kid," Kane went on, as if that explained everything. He gripped Rachel's waist more firmly and turned her around so their eyes met. "Mariette and Mel want her to go to Juilliard in the fall, and she's determined to go out on her own. I guess the whole thing finally came to a head."

"So naturally she hopped in her car and drove four hundred miles to talk it over with you."

"She looks up to me, Rachel," he said evenly.

"That isn't hard for her, I'm sure. I'd say she's all of five foot four in those heels."

One brow quirked upward. "I believe you're jealous."

"Don't flatter yourself."

His grip loosened on her waist, and Rachel pulled away. Side-stepping him, she got the berries from the table and went back to the sink to dump them in the colander. When she reached for the faucet, Kane's hand came out to imprison hers.

"Who's acting like a child now?" he taunted. His tone reminded her far too much of the one he had used with Victoria just moments before. Patronizing. Indulgent. Who the hell did he think he was?

"Why don't they let her finish high school first before Mariette and Mel worry about packing her off to Juilliard?" Rachel shook off his hand and flipped on the cold water.

"She graduated a year early. Vicky's a very bright girl, Rachel."

"Oh, I can see that," Rachel snapped, fingers swiftly picking through the dark fruit.

"You've never heard her sing. She has an incredible talent. Mariette's aware of it, of course. But as a mother, she's also justifiably worried about the problems that come with a career in the music business. She wouldn't want to see Vicky get in too deep before she can handle it."

"And where do you fit in?" Rachel asked flatly, hoping he couldn't tell how important his answer was.

Kane leaned against the counter, considering. He seemed a million miles away from her at that moment, caught up in his concern for the girl whose soft, crushed-velvet voice could be heard faintly above them.

"I only know she's got what it takes to make it. She's . . . special. A perfect ear, strong in the upper register, but she's actually an alto. And the quality of her voice . . . it's really indescribable. You'll have to hear it. It wraps around you and takes you . . . where a song was meant to go."

Rachel focused on the brisk movements of her own hands beneath the running water. Sorting, rinsing, picking off a clinging stem. *And where do I fit in?* she wanted to ask. It began to seem more and more clear why he hadn't brought up again the subject of their future together.

A sideways glance told Rachel she needn't worry that Kane would sense the direction of her thoughts. His mind was on the clicking heels at the top of the stairs.

Kane no longer lounged against the counter. He was all nervous energy now, striding across the floor to meet Victoria as she descended.

"Well?"

The girl held up a small box. "Are these for me?" Her face wore the expression of an excited child at Christmas.

Kane glowered down at her. "Didn't Mariette ever tell you it's rude to go through people's drawers?"

Victoria tried to appear chastened. "Well, the drawer was partway open. I was just going to close it when I saw the box. And you do always get me earrings because you know how I love them and so I thought—"

"Yes," Kane cut in with an impatient nod. "They're for you."

Victoria laughed gaily and began tugging the tinkling gold chimes from her ears.

"Now what did your mother say?" Kane pressed on.

Rachel could tell that his attempt at a scowl was only a half-hearted effort to mask the anxious tenderness that moved in his eyes. She snapped her attention back to the sink and flipped off the faucet with an angry jerk. Grasping the colander by the handles, she shook the excess water from it none too gently.

"She's not exactly happy," Victoria said in her husky woman's voice. "She says it's all right if I stay for a few days, though. If you don't mind having me around."

Kane let out an exasperated sigh. Rachel refused to watch this exchange, but she knew the gesture that accompanied the sigh; he would be raking a hand back through his hair.

"I think she figures you'll talk some sense into me." Victoria trilled out a dulcet laugh. "She still doesn't realize you're on my side." Rachel stared out the window. "You are on my side, aren't you?"

"I never take sides." The reply was too hasty to be convincing.

There was a silence. Rachel left the colander in the sink and went to the paper bag. She might as well leave them the vegetables. Gran had plenty in the garden, and it was silly to take them back. In her determination to keep moving, she almost tripped over Nat, who was sprawled on the floor beside the table. He looked up at her with the saddest, most hangdog expression she had ever seen. Perhaps he didn't like what was going on here any more than Rachel did.

"Can we get my suitcases now?" Victoria broke the silence at last. "And what about lunch? I'm starved."

Another silence. Rachel pulled open the refrigerator and stared with unseeing eyes at the bright coldness within.

"See if Rachel can use your help," Kane said curtly. Seconds later the front door closed.

Rachel knelt and put the lettuce in the crisper. When she crossed back to the table for the rest of the vegetables, Victoria was still standing at the foot of the stairs, staring off dreamily in the general direction of the door. The girl seemed to sense Rachel's glance and turned.

"He really likes this country stuff, doesn't he?" The violet gaze flicked over the spare, cedar-accented room to light briefly on Rachel's too-large T-shirt and faded jeans.

Rachel picked up the vegetables and went back to the refrigerator. "Kane likes variety. Period," she muttered pointedly, carefully tucking the spears of asparagus beside the lettuce. There was no reason to take her frustration out on the vegetables.

Vegetables. Rachel almost laughed. When she got back to L.A. she would be thinking a lot about them. There was Elaine and the proposal for Mariette to deal with, after all. Would Rachel be dreaming up a clever way to combine artichokes and cabbage leaves into an amusing centerpiece for the mother while the daughter studied with the masters at Juilliard—or worked intensively with Kane on developing that "incredible talent"?

Victoria was at the table now, making herself comfortable in a chair. Allowing one of the sleek high heels to slide off, she nuzzled the dog with a graceful foot. Nat sighed contentedly and closed his eyes. *You traitor*, Rachel thought, indulging herself in a grim smile.

"What can I do to help?" Victoria asked, stretching her arms over her head lazily, giving a slight yawn. High, pert breasts strained against the fabric of her blouse. The earrings Rachel had watched Kane buy on the Fourth of July dangled enchantingly, a fetching concoction of raven feathers and mother of pearl against the ebony fall of her hair.

Rachel wanted to slap the satisfied grin from the heart-shaped face. But she had to admit the earrings looked lovely, and it wasn't her concern if the girl was spoiled, used to being waited on. Victoria Sayer had obviously been handed anything she wanted on a silver platter from the time she could crawl.

"There's nothing to do," Rachel replied tightly, taking a tray of already-sliced cheeses and fruit from the top shelf of the refrigerator.

The front door opened, and Kane came back in, lugging two large suitcases and a smaller overnight case. It was clear that Victoria planned to be well dressed in her role of runaway. And why not? Running away from home was a risky business. Victoria would want to be prepared for anything that might pop up, an impromptu interview with the local juvenile authorities, or a hot date for dinner at Sardine Lake.

At a glowering look from Kane on his way to the stairs, Victoria slid her shoe back on and stood up. "I guess I'll set the table," she said grudgingly.

Rachel said nothing, allowing the girl to fumble around in the cupboards for glasses and small plates. *Just get through this lunch*, Rachel instructed herself, *then you can leave without making a scene.* Her mind raced wildly. She needed an excuse to get away that wouldn't arouse suspicion. It shouldn't be too difficult. Victoria would be glad to see her go, and Kane clearly had not given her a thought since the younger girl's arrival.

The meal seemed interminable. Victoria babbled on about some promoter who had promised her a recording contract. Kane's comments were terse and more than a little gruff. He was waiting, Rachel knew, for her to be gone—so he could be alone with this black-haired child.

Rachel felt her anger rise, tried to control it by nibbling on a wedge of creamy Camembert. The cheese had all the flavor of a gum eraser.

So he'd had the mother. Had a lot of mileage out of her, too. Now it was on to fresher pickings. After a harmless detour, of course, for a meaningless encounter with a long-forgotten old flame.

Victoria was getting up from the table and going over to the fireplace where the old Gibson leaned against the stones. "Let's go out on the deck." She smiled invitingly.

They're going to sing together now, Rachel thought, *and I'm not sticking around to hear it.*

A knife-point of pain stabbed through her building rage. Kane had achieved success now, but he hadn't done it with his songs. That had been his first dream, after all. And if Victoria had the voice he claimed . . .

"Rachel and I were going on a hike," Kane said.

"No. . . ." Without thinking, Rachel laid a hand on his arm. She snatched it back when she touched the warm, taut flesh. "I forgot to tell you. Sarah called. She wondered if I could watch Johnny this afternoon. She has a . . . doctor's appointment in Grass Valley."

Kane was looking at her now, perhaps a little suspiciously. But wasn't there also just the faintest shadow of relief in the near-black eyes?

"You didn't mention it before."

"Really, Kane," said Victoria with ill-disguised impatience. "If she has to go, she has to go."

"Shut up, Victoria," Kane ordered blankly.

The girl froze and looked down at her grown-up shoes. That was cruel of him, Rachel thought, suddenly feeling a twinge of pity for this tiny woman-child. What did a seventeen-year-old know about handling a man like Kane Walker?

"I . . . I'm sorry." Victoria looked up, eyes treacherously moist.

"It's all right," Rachel said softly, coming to her feet. "I know you two have a lot to talk about. And I do have to be going."

Victoria rushed into the social amenities. "It was really great to see you again, Miss Davis. Maybe we can have a barbecue or something before—"

"For heaven's sake, call me Rachel!" She knew she'd spoken harshly. But if the girl called her Miss Davis one more time, Rachel was going to scream. She longed to bolt for the door. But that would never do.

"I certainly hope everything works out for you," Rachel said, wondering vaguely if she was achieving any degree of sincerity at all. "Kane says you're very talented."

"He does?" The tapering hands reached for the guitar.

Rachel forced the corners of her mouth to turn up and managed a curt nod. Her reward was a dazzling smile from Victoria.

"C'mon, Nat." Rachel slapped her thigh, and the dog was at her side. Ignoring the scraping of a chair behind her at the table, she made it to the door and out to her Mercedes.

Nat leaped onto the seat readily. Rachel was behind the wheel and fumbling with her keys before Kane caught up with her.

"What was that all about?" He was leaning into the open window, his brows drawn together in an expression that managed to appear both exasperated and solicitous at the same time.

"I really have to go, Kane." Her insides were churning. If he would only back away from the window . . .

"Rachel."

"Would you please just don't . . . Rachel me."

"I know Victoria can be a hopeless brat sometimes. But it's just a cover-up. Underneath she's confused and just a little bit scared. You'll get along fine with her when you get to know her better."

Oh, he was a pro at handling women. He didn't miss a trick.

Faintly, from the deck on the other side of the house, Victoria strummed the guitar. Kane reached through the window and laid a hand against Rachel's cheek.

"What is it?" he asked coaxingly.

Rachel jerked away. "Would you mind stepping back from the car?"

"Talk to me. Tell me . . ." he began very low.

"What?" she asked. "That I'll be waiting by the phone for you to call when you can fit me in? That I had a wonderful time, and maybe we can do it again in another six years? That it's perfectly natural for you to want the daughter after all you got out of Mariette?"

Beneath the healthy tan, his face went dead white. "What's got into you? I thought . . ."

"What?" she glared at him defiantly. "That I'd conveniently turn my back while you make love to a little girl in high-heeled shoes? You'd better be careful this time, Kane. Fooling around with jailbait can be dangerous!"

He was staring at her as if she'd suddenly sprouted horns. "You're the same heartless bitch you were before!" He spat the words at her. "Ready to accuse me of anything. From screwing the best friend a man could have to seducing her innocent daughter."

"Get your hands off my car!"

"God, I've been a fool . . . to think that you could change!" His fingers gripped the window's edge in white-knuckled fury. "You'll never change. You'll hide behind some deep and buried fear until the day you die."

He leaned in closer, his rage seeming to burn the very air around her. She cringed away, but there was no escape. "What is the fear, Rachel? That love equals loss? That Daddy left and Mommy left and anyone you dare to love will do the same?"

Blindly Rachel fumbled with the keys again. His hand shot through the open window and closed around her wrist. With a muffled clink the keys dropped to her lap.

"I'm not finished yet. . . ."

Rachel opened her mouth. No words would come. If only he would step back. Just get out of the way so she could leave. Her wrist felt numb and nerveless in his grip, like the rest of her.

"I haven't pushed you since that day at the Cliffs. I've told myself that you really did care for me, even if you couldn't find the words to say it. But you're not capable of loving, are you? Because love might mean you'd have to trust someone. And your cold, dead heart never learned how!"

She wouldn't move. If she sat still enough, soon he would release her.

The moment stretched into infinity. Very close, a dog whimpered. Nat. It must be Nat. There were . . . birds singing. As if it were a very ordinary day. And the guitar. Victoria was playing the guitar somewhere far away.

Victoria began to sing. Even muted by the distance and the sturdy cabin walls, the voice was all that Kane had promised. Rich, husky but somehow pure and true. It reached out invisible tendrils of sound composed of equal parts: merciless pain, unbearable beauty.

Not yet morning when I left you
locked behind your wall of dreams.
There was nothing I could tell you
that you would believe.

Are there hurts too deep for healing?
Do you weave them into spells?
There was so much more I wanted,
but you don't believe . . .

"Rachel, I . . ." he got out on a torn breath. He had released her wrist. She rubbed at it absently. "She must have heard me sing it. I swear I never—"

"No. Please. No excuses. She . . . does it justice." Rachel retrieved the keys from her lap.

Kane made no move to stop her this time when she stuck the right one in the ignition and gave it a turn. The engine fired and hummed obediently.

He seemed to fade backward from the door. A ghost, a long-lost love, glimpsed briefly in a fading dream.

"Goodbye, Kane," she said softly.

He watched her, hands stuffed in his pockets, as she drove away.

12

ON THE OTHER SIDE of the kitchen door, Nat scratched softly. Rachel glanced at the clock on the stove. After seven. She had been sitting at the table staring off into space for over an hour. By rote she went to the service porch and loaded up the dog's bowl with dry food, mixing it with some from a can to give it flavor.

Her hands were really a mess, she noticed numbly as she laid the bowl in front of the dog. She hadn't given them a thought since the night they'd gone up to the Lakes. The bronze polish was all cracked. Chipped. Lucinda, the manicurist she went to regularly in L.A., would have a fit.

But L.A. seemed very far away; her carefully constructed life there, somehow hollow at the core. She would have to go back soon, she knew. Perhaps some of the usual savor would return to it all when she picked up the threads of the well-remembered pattern and worked diligently once again at weaving them into a whole. Maybe she would open an office in San Francisco. Illusions Unlimited was already building a significant client list in the Bay Area. And it was expensive, trucking everything up there. It would be nice, too, to be near Catherine. Kane had opened a Centrifugal Force in San Francisco, and it had done quite well. As had the one in San Diego. . . .

Rachel shook her head. Kane again. All her thoughts led back to him. He had successfully invaded every corner of her life.

Rachel wandered into Gran's room. There was the faintest hint of lavender in the close air. Gran's scent. If only Gran were here! Rachel would lay her head against the broad bosom and feel the strong old hands stroking her hair.

Fleetingly, in the full-length mirror on the wall, she caught a glimpse of Lydia. The haunted face, framed by the dark wild-curled cloud of hair, stared out at her reproachfully.

Rachel reached out a trembling hand. Cold glass. Her own reflection. She was her mother's daughter, after all. Not incapable of love, as Kane had accused, but terrified of it. A faint, twisted smile curved the lips of her image. He had been right about the other part, though; to her, love between a man and a woman had always been a neat, mathematical formula: love equals loss. And once again, the formula had proven true. True, at least in part, because she herself had made it so. She hadn't trusted him. Or she would have known him innocent with Victoria.

But was he innocent? If he had fallen in love with one so young, it would be natural for him to fight it, perhaps even to the extent of resurrecting an old love and pursuing her relentlessly in a hopeless attempt to forget the child.

Could he be that cruel? Did he consider Rachel fair game after the way she'd hurt him before? Did he think of her as shallow and hard, irrationally jealous of the women whose bodies he worked to transform and totally unsupportive when it came to his dreams for a career as a songwriter?

Rachel pressed tense fingers to her pounding temples. Oh, it was all too much. "If this is love," she murmured aloud with unexpected humor, "then no wonder my mother wanted nothing to do with it."

It was half an hour later, when she sat in Gran's rocking chair with a steaming cup of tea to soothe her, that Rachel realized she had thought of Lydia as her mother for the first time in almost twenty years. It wasn't so difficult now, in the depths of her own confusion, to comprehend how her mother must have felt, married to a passionate, possessive stranger at nineteen, swept off to a world in which she was an outsider, shackled more tightly to a life she hated when she bore a child a few months later.

In the quiet room the rocker creaked a comforting, familiar rhythm. Rachel allowed herself to imagine that the woman who had given her birth was with her now. Not the tortured, love-ravaged creature Rachel had known in childhood, but the woman her mother might have become had she lived, a woman tempered by time and hard-won understanding to a powerful, earth-born wisdom.

Rachel could almost see her, strong and tall, dressed in sturdy denim pants and a soft flannel shirt, her eyes that sunlit forest green. Perhaps her hair would have gray at the temples, flowing out into the rich and tangled darkness like the paths of silvered rivers on rolling terrain.

Her mother, holding out her arms. Rachel moving into them, clasped for a moment in a fierce maternal embrace that was at once all the hugs and kisses never given, all the tender love words never shared.

Rachel knew it was a fantasy, but she indulged in it nonetheless. It was a benediction, a loosening and falling away of the last constricting knot that bound her to the inchoate turmoil of her childhood. What remained was the knowledge that Catherine had been too proud to show her love, her mother too much in pain and her father simply—too late.

It was a pattern. And for the first time Rachel saw it clearly. She had woven it herself from the partial understanding that tied her to the past. Pride and the pain of old wounds had kept her from telling Kane she loved him over these past few golden days, had held her back from revealing to him all the destructive doubts that filled her head.

The possibility that the entire cycle had been traversed—that it was now too late—galvanized her into action. She would do it, would give herself—and Kane— a chance. Perhaps the truth he would tell her would not be what she longed to hear. But she would bear it somehow and garner strength from the test of facing down those lifelong demons. This time she would not lose her love to silence and the twisted, lonely torture of conjecture that came after.

The smooth black mouthpiece of the phone was in her hands. She dialed hastily, not giving herself time to reconsider.

The line was busy. She would wait a few minutes and try again. The tea was still warm. Rachel poured herself another cup, added sugar and drank it standing up, pacing nervously, anxious to reach him before she lost her nerve.

The second try yielded the same results, as did a third an hour later. Maybe he had taken it off the hook.... She would simply not allow herself to consider what the blaring, relentless busy signal might mean. She'd had enough of dealing in unsubstantiated assumptions.

It would have to wait until tomorrow. And she wouldn't call. She would go to him. Tell him everything, with the hapless Victoria as witness, if need be.

There was nothing more to do until morning. Rachel drew a bath and removed the chipped polish from her nails, all the while rehearsing little speeches to herself in the bathroom mirror, reminding herself of all she must tell him, sure she was going to make a fool of herself but determined to hold on to her resolve. She soaked for over an hour, lathering and rinsing her hair twice and leaving the conditioner on for the full twenty-five minutes specified on the bottle. It was past midnight when she climbed wearily into bed.

The tired, strained face that confronted her in the mirror the next morning made Rachel long to drag herself back up the stairs and burrow deeply beneath the tousled pile of blankets.

Instead she ran her hands lightly down her hips, smoothing out imaginary wrinkles in the snug-fitting magenta designer jeans. With a reassuring nod she told herself that the dolman-sleeved pale fuchsia pullover had always looked wonderful on her. She would brew herself a nice strong cup of coffee and then spend at least half an hour making up her face. But first she would pick a new rosebud for the bottle on the windowsill.

Rachel took a pair of scissors from a kitchen drawer and went out the side door. It was a beautiful morning, already warm. A steady wind was blowing from the south.

At the top of the steps leading down to the front yard she glanced up at Grizzly Peak. To the left of the stony crags, in the hills behind the post office, a thick, billowing cloud of smoke rose to taint the pristine summer sky.

There was a truck approaching from the Old Road. It was Billy Short, driving a little too fast. Rachel ran out to the street and flagged him down.

Billy slammed on the brakes and managed to skid to a stop a few feet in front of Rachel. "Jeez, Rachel. You're lucky I got lightnin' reflexes. What'd you want to go and do a fool thing like that for?" Billy attempted a glare around the stub of a cold, well-chewed cigar. The head of the little plastic dog on the cluttered dashboard was bobbing up and down.

"I saw the fire. Where is it? Is it . . . I mean . . . ?"

"Past the County Works. Up Goodyears Creek Road. I'm headin' up there now." Billy impatiently fingered the gearshift knob. But when Rachel didn't step back, he indulged in a knowing grin, careful to keep the cigar clutched firmly between tobacco-stained teeth. "Looks like it's gettin' away from 'em," he said.

"Who?" Rachel asked weakly.

"Forest Service. Who d'you think?" Billy granted her a condescending snort. "The wind's up, Rachel. Or ain't you noticed?" Billy licked a greased, creased finger and stuck it out the window and up in the air. "Yessir. Blowin' north. Came up about an hour ago. 'Til then they just had the Marley cabin to worry about."

"The Marley cabin?"

"The one right on the other side of the bridge past the County Works. Caught fire 'bout six this mornin'. They ain't figured out how yet. But that old place is a fire trap, anyway. All boarded up since Old Man Marley died. You know which one I mean? Kinda stuck in a corner right before the road swerves left and up to the— Er...Rachel, you feelin' all right?"

"I'm fine. The fire's moving up the hill...to the north?"

"Yep. I figure I'll go up and give 'em a hand. Not that anyone'll appreciate it. Seems like, these days, them Forest Service guys think they know it all. But I coulda told 'em they shoulda done somethin' 'fore now 'bout that place. Old boards're dry as tinder, and we ain't had rain since May." Billy took the cold cigar from between his teeth and flicked a nonexistent ash onto the floorboards beside him.

"Did everyone up Goodyears Creek Road get down all right?" Rachel asked carefully.

"Now Rachel, I ain't no psychic, y'know. When the wind turns like that, things can happen pretty damn fast." He was looking at her somewhat warily. "Er...maybe you oughtta go and lie down or somethin'. You're lookin' a little green around the gills."

"But there's no other way off the hill, is there?" Rachel demanded impatiently.

"Well, no," Billy conceded. "Except to take off on foot through some pretty rough country. But with the head of the fire at your back, that'd be a damn fool thing to do. Seein' as how you'd have not only the surface fire to worry about, but the crown fires spreadin' in the branches up above. And if the wind keeps up, the sparks'll be startin' up spot fires all around." Billy shifted the cigar to the other corner of his mouth. "Yessir. Any fool who lets himself get trapped up there is gonna need some luck to keep from bein' crispy-fied!"

"Can you give me a ride?" Her voice sounded unnaturally high to her own ears.

"Now Rachel, you'll just be in the way. This here's a job for the men." Billy patted her hand awkwardly.

"Then I'll have to take my own car," Rachel said quietly, already turning away. This was no time to give in to rising hysteria. Or to take Billy Short to task for his infuriating chauvinism.

"Well, I guess if you're gonna go, anyway..." Billy drawled consideringly.

Rachel ran around to the passenger side and jumped in. They were halfway up the cut, a pair of foam rubber dice bouncing merrily beneath the rearview mirror, before Rachel remembered she hadn't locked the doors. The pair of scissors was still clutched tightly in her hand. She set them on the dashboard, right beside the bobbly-headed plastic dog.

The Goodyears Creek Road was blocked off, guarded with uncompromising efficiency by several Forest Service men in khaki uniforms. Though there would be no danger until past the bridge, they were taking no chances. The fire hadn't burned up the hill enough to be really visible, she noticed. There was just the smoke, a distance to the north up the road.

Ignoring the signals to turn around waved by the men in green, Billy pulled off onto the shoulder, flung open his door and swung his beefy body to the ground. He seemed to have completely forgotten his passenger as he strolled over to engage in a lively argument with one of the men who had waved them back.

Rachel got out of the truck. Ruth Daniels, who lived up the road in a house below Kane's, came up beside her and took her arm.

"There's nothing to worry about, Rachel. They'll have it under control soon, I'm sure."

"Is . . . everybody off the hill?"

"Bob and I got down half an hour ago." Ruth gestured toward a blue sedan. Beside it stood Bob Daniels. He was talking to a balding man with a little girl clutching his hand. "That's Andre Garnica. He was here when we got here." She indicated several other people, standing in groups near their cars, all looking a little bewildered, speaking to each other in low voices. "Most everybody else is here, I think—"

"Kane Walker?" Rachel asked on a rising inflection.

"I . . . we haven't seen him," Ruth confessed. "But he's pretty high up. They're leading everybody down. Don't worry." Ruth smiled reassuringly. "The road was still passable when we went through. I'm sure he'll be here soon."

The wind was at Rachel's back, blowing strands of hair into her mouth. Rachel swiped them away impatiently. From above came the sound of helicopters, their steady, chopping blades beating more loudly as they passed over, fading as they went beyond and toward the fire.

"They're doing everything they can," Ruth continued in a low, nervous tone that told Rachel the older woman was really trying to convince herself. One after another, the helicopters discharged shimmering falls of liquid onto the roiling clouds of smoke below them.

Billy jogged over, having concluded his enthusiastic, gesticulating exchange with the blockade guard. "They got plenty of ground equipment up there already," he announced expansively. "They're havin' some trouble establishin' a fire line, though, on account of there ain't no clear spaces to work from. But they got everybody down and they also got the . . . utmost confidence that they'll have it under control soon without undue damage to property, either private or public." Billy beamed proudly, clearly pleased to have remembered every word the ranger had told him. Ruth shot him a grim look and went to stand beside her husband.

A truck came into view, approaching from the far side of the blockade. It stopped just short of the barrier to drop off two passengers: Kane and Victoria.

Relief exploded inside Rachel. He was all right! He hadn't been hurt, he was out of danger!

"What'd I tell you," Billy said smugly, as if he himself had been responsible for the timely actions of the Forest Service. "Got every one of 'em down without a hitch."

But Rachel hardly heard him. There was no one in the world but the man in khaki pants and lace-up boots. His back was to her now; he was talking to one of the rangers. But when he turned . . . she would be there for him. She had so much to tell him, so much to share. When he turned, he would know that she was ready at last to love and be loved in return. When he turned . . .

Victoria, at least, had seen her. The girl was looking lost and more than a little out of place in a hot-pink sweatshirt minidress and a pair of black patent-leather heels. She was clutching Kane's guitar. Rachel raised a tentative hand. The girl's eyes slid away.

Leaving Billy babbling on about line crews and backfiring techniques, Rachel walked slowly down to the blockade. Perhaps she had been mistaken, and Victoria hadn't caught sight of her, after all. Rachel was close enough now to hear Victoria's frightened voice as she grabbed Kane's arm.

"Oh, Kane. I was so terrified. Hold me. Hold me, please...."

Kane wrapped both arms around the girl. The guitar made a hollow sound as it bumped against his leg. "It's all right, little one," he crooned. "It's over now."

The ranger cleared his throat and made a pretense of talking into his handheld radio.

"I . . . I guess it's just hitting me now," the girl sobbed brokenly. "The heat of it. I never felt heat like that before. Like it could suck the blood right out of your body. And we drove right through the middle of it— And what about your house? What if it . . . ?"

Kane stroked the blue-black hair. "A house can be rebuilt," he reminded the girl in a low, half-teasing voice. Then he grasped her by the shoulders and held her away from him enough so that he could look into her uptilted, tearstained face.

Victoria sniffled bravely. "They could have at least let us drive our cars down. If anything happens to that MG, Daddy is going to—"

"It was safer to ride down with the ranger," Kane cut in patiently. "Now. The thing for us to do is get you into Downieville. It's going to be several hours at least before we can go back up that road. I'll arrange for a hotel room and then—"

"That won't be necessary," Rachel said in a clear, firm voice. "Victoria can come with me to Gran's."

Kane's back stiffened as if Rachel's words had hit him between the shoulder blades. Then he allowed himself to turn and look at her. Something flared in the brown-black depths of his eyes and was as quickly extinguished. His gaze moved over her assessingly before he nodded his head.

"If it won't inconvenience you," he said coldly.

Rachel shrugged. "Not at all. I'll fix us both some breakfast, and then we can have a nice long talk."

"But Kane . . ." Victoria was giving him the full treatment, lashes fluttering wildly, hands clutching in ardent supplication.

"No buts." It was a command. "Rachel will look out for you until—"

"I don't need anyone to look out for me! Especially her!" Victoria's ears had turned the same hot pink as the enamel hearts that graced them.

"You're behaving like a spoiled child, Vicky. You keep telling me how grown up you are. For heaven's sake, why don't you act like it?"

"I won't go with her! I won't!"

Rachel cast a glance at the forest ranger, who had finished his conversation on the little radio and was staring intently at his heavy-duty boots. Over by the blue sedan, the small group of people that included Ruth Daniels was trying hard not to eavesdrop.

"And you can't make me!" Victoria screamed. "I can do what I want, and I want to stay here!"

Kane seemed unable to decide whether to stifle the girl with a hand over her mouth or turn her across his knees.

"Maybe it would be better if—" Rachel began in an effort to be diplomatic.

"She's going with you!" Kane boomed threateningly.

"I'm not! I'm not!" Victoria beat her fists on Kane's chest.

Billy Short saved the day. "Only one way to handle a hysterical woman," he commented sagely as he leaped the blockade. He grabbed Victoria away from Kane and slung her over his shoulder. "Come on, Rachel. I'll drive you home."

Victoria continued to yelp and protest, beating at Billy with ineffectual fists as he carried her, a squirming bundle of pink sweatshirt and flailing legs, toward the truck.

Kane stared after them, relief and amusement fighting for precedence on his face. He caught Rachel watching him covertly, and his expression resolved itself into a taunting grin.

"Sorry about that, Rachel. I know how you hate a scene."

13

KANE'S GUITAR LEANED against the wall beside the couch on which Victoria huddled, clutching her knees. Black patent-leather heels lay discarded on the floor beneath the coffee table. The hot pink minidress had ridden dangerously high on her thighs, but Victoria couldn't have cared less.

At the counter, Rachel sliced a loaf of homemade bread. "One egg or two?" she asked brightly.

"I never eat breakfast," was the surly response.

Rachel smiled. "Then I'll just cook you one."

There was a mutinous silence. Rachel popped the bread into the toaster and cracked three eggs in a cast-iron pan.

Victoria burst into tears. Rachel turned off the flame under the eggs and took the box of tissue from the windowsill. "Here," she said, holding out the box.

Victoria grabbed a handful of tissue and addressed the bookcase. "He doesn't love me. He thinks of me like a . . . kid sister!" Great, racking sobs shook her frail shoulders.

Rachel sank to the couch and laid the box of tissue on the coffee table. "I think he loves you a great deal," she said softly.

"Yeah. Sure." Rachel was granted a withering glare that dissolved in another flood of tears. "But not like he loves you. He's always loved you. And you...you treated him like dirt!"

"Is that what he told you?"

"No! He...he never tells me anything. But everybody knows how he feels about you. I know he wrote that song for you. It's one of his best songs, and he wouldn't even teach it to me."

"He should have."

"Wh-what?"

"You sing it beautifully. The song may have been written for me. But it was meant for you to sing."

The violet eyes lit up briefly before the veil of mistrust descended again. "You're treating me like a kid. Everybody treats me like a baby. Well, I'm not." Lowering her legs to the floor, Victoria tugged at the hem of the minidress and sat up very straight. "Now my mother's coming to get me. She doesn't trust me to come home by myself, so she's coming to get me like I was a kid."

"But when you spoke with her on the phone—"

"Oh, you're so dumb." The husky voice did its best to sound contemptuous. "I never called her. I just pretended to. She wouldn't let me stay here when Kane is trying to get back with you. She thinks I'd just be in the way."

The tapering hands began tearing little strips off the hapless wad of tissue. "But Kane figured it out after you left. He called her himself last night. They had a two-hour conference about me while I sat there waiting for them to decide what to do. It was humiliating."

Rachel handed her a fresh tissue. Victoria set the soggy wad of used ones on the coffee table and blew her nose. "So now I'll be sent off to Juilliard, and everybody will be glad to get rid of me, and you can have Kane all to yourself."

"Oh, Victoria . . ." Rachel grabbed the girl by her proud, thin shoulders and gathered her into her arms.

"Don't touch me. . . ."

Rachel held on. In the end, Victoria allowed herself to be comforted. "You've got everything. I hate you," she sniffed between sobs.

Rachel didn't reply, only held the small, warm body of the girl close until she quieted.

"I guess you . . . hate me, too?" Victoria murmured tremulously when the worst of the sobbing was past.

"No." Rachel grinned, shaking her head. "I may envy you a little, but I certainly don't hate you."

"How can you envy me? I've made a mess of everything, and I lied, and I—"

"But you told the truth just now. I don't know if I'd have had the courage to do that."

"Courage? It doesn't take courage to cry like a baby."

"I think you're wrong there. And I know it took courage to confess you think Kane's in love with me."

Victoria blew her nose again. Then the violet eyes narrowed measuringly.

"You really mean that."

"I do."

"Something's different about you."

"Maybe I've finally grown up."

"How old are you, anyway?"

"Twenty-nine."

"That's pretty old to be just growing up."

Rachel wrinkled her nose. "I'm a late bloomer."

"God. I guess so." Victoria drew her knees back up under her and flipped a waterfall of black hair over her shoulder. "If you and Kane get . . . work things out . . . would you be jealous if I still sing his songs?"

"No matter what happens, it would be a crime for you not to sing them. You may consider me a rival. But even a rival can tell great talent when she hears it. I know you have a fine career ahead of you, Juilliard or not. Kane's songs are meant to be a part of it."

Victoria was pulling at the hem of her dress again. When it refused to stretch over her knees, she gave a small sigh and swiped at her nose with the back of her hand. "I'm not your rival," she mumbled. "Kane belongs to you. He always has."

"I wouldn't be too sure about that," Rachel countered with a wry smile.

Victoria flopped back against the couch cushions and let out an exaggerated groan. "I don't believe it! I mean, I may only be seventeen, but even I can see the nose on my face when I look in the mirror. You actually have doubts? About Kane? Why do you think he still wears that ring you gave him? And why else would he go and build a cabin four hundred miles from L.A.?"

"He loves it here. He has since—"

"Trees are trees," Victoria snapped tartly. "Oh, I know, I know. You think this is the most beautiful country on earth and all that. But you have to admit, there are plenty of trees in California. And a lot of them are south of Bakersfield. And weren't you just a little bit suspicious when he showed up here for his vacation at exactly the same time you were taking yours?"

"I was, but I thought—"

"You can be pretty dense, you know?"

"But I—"

"Look, do we have to talk about it anymore? It hasn't been an easy morning for me. You know?"

"Victoria, if you're so sure Kane's still in love with me, then why did you behave the way you have?"

"So I'm jealous. Haven't you ever been jealous?"

Rachel cleared her throat. "Well, I . . ."

"And the minute you walked in the door of his cabin. . . . You have to understand. I never saw you like that before. You were always so perfect in L.A. I always thought of you in cream-colored silk with your hair pulled back, telling a bunch of frantic workpeople where to put things in that calm, low voice you have.

"But then yesterday you were . . . someone different. With your vegetables and your berries and those hiking boots. The lace-up kind. Just like Kane's. I knew then I didn't have a chance, that I never had had a chance. And it made me mad. I'm still a little mad, if you want to know the truth."

"But you had me believing—"

"I know, I know. God. I thought *I* was insecure. Maybe I will have an egg, after all."

Rachel realized the subject was closed when Victoria padded over to the stove and turned the flame back on under the eggs.

MARIETTE AND MEL SAYER arrived in a rented car at two that afternoon. They had already spoken with Kane, who was still up at the blockade.

The wind had died down, and the fire was under control. No homes had been destroyed, but a stray spark had ignited Andre Garnica's garage, and the roof had been lost before the flames could be doused. Weather permitting, the homeowners would be back in their houses by evening.

Mel was anxious to get back to L.A., where he was in the midst of "delicate negotiations" concerning his upcoming film. He left Mariette with his daughter, reasoning that the fire danger was past and they would have the MG to take them home.

Rachel said a silent prayer that the city-bred producer's logic would hold true. Fire danger was never really past in this country of thick, close-growing evergreens, not until the last ember was long cold. And even then a thoughtless cigarette or an untended campfire could spell disaster once again.

Rachel drove to Downieville to pick up a few groceries. It was just an excuse, really, to let Mariette and Victoria have some time alone. When she returned, Victoria was uncharacteristically subdued. Mariette looked as if she could use either a Scotch on the rocks or a nice, hot bath. Rachel offered the latter. Mariette sighed gratefully and took the flowered towel Rachel handed her.

The three women shared a dinner of broiled trout and wild rice. Mariette did her best to keep the desultory conversation going, but Rachel kept wondering what was happening at the blockade. Victoria pushed the grains of rice around on her plate and picked at the sweet white meat. To dispel the rather gloomy mood, Rachel suggested a walk when they'd finished the meal.

Victoria waved a hand in the direction of Gran's bookcase. "I've seen enough trees for a while. If it's okay with you guys, I'll stay here and snoop around in some of these books." She attempted an enthusiastic smile. "You know, your grandmother must be some old lady. She's even got the *Encyclopedia of Rock and Roll* here."

"She belongs to at least ten book clubs," Rachel explained. "She's always getting books in the mail. If they look at all intriguing, she keeps them." Rachel turned to Victoria's mother. "Mariette? Feel like looking at trees?" She fully expected another excuse.

Mariette surprised her. "I'd love to," she said, sounding grateful to get out of the house.

With Nat bouncing along beside them, they took the road that led past the Bachels' Hotel toward the bridge over Woodruff Creek. Rachel played tour guide, pointing out that the hotel had been built in 1864 and was now a private residence, that the road past Woodruff Creek Bridge led eventually to the site where the Mountain House, an important inn and stage station, had once stood.

"It was famous for miles around," Rachel told Mariette as they stood on the small bridge and gazed over the edge at the waters of the creek below. "They even had grand balls there, complete with a brass band, once a year." Rachel looked up to find violet eyes regarding her steadily. "I . . . excuse me. Maybe you aren't in the mood for a history lesson."

Mariette's softly curving lips spread into a smile. "I admit I've got a few things on my mind. Actually, I was hoping my daughter hasn't caused too many problems."

Rachel sighed. "No problems that didn't need to be faced long before she arrived on the scene." Down below, a trout leaped from the water after a dragonfly, its belly gleaming whitely before it was gone again with a small splash. Rachel knew there was more to be said. "Mariette, I . . ."

Mariette took her arm. "It's getting dark. Shall we go back?"

They turned together and retraced their steps in silence for a time. But Rachel knew she owed the woman beside her an apology. And who could tell when she'd have another chance to give it?

Her own voice sounded strained as she gathered the nerve to make her confession. "Mariette, I think I owe you an..."

"Apology?" Mariette said softly, sensing her train of thought. Rachel gulped and opened her mouth to speak again, but Mariette wasn't finished. "Maybe you do."

"I—"

"If you don't mind, I have something I'd like to say before you go further."

"All right." Rachel was slightly taken aback by the other woman's suddenly crisp tone.

"As far as saying you're sorry to me for any...hasty assumptions you might have drawn about my relationship with Kane—" Rachel shot her a wide-eyed glance "—of course I knew what you thought, even though Kane was as tight as a clam when it came to talking about you. After all, you did send me that curt little note about regretting that your services would no longer be available for any future events I might be planning."

Rachel had the grace to blush. Mariette continued. "Anyway, as far as your belief that Kane and I were having an affair, it's obvious you've come to your senses on that score. And I simply don't have the negative energy it takes to harbor unnecessary grudges. So let's say I accept your apology with relief and respect that you've got the guts to admit you were wrong."

"Well. Thanks," Rachel said numbly.

They were passing the turnoff that led across the river and up the cut. Mariette glanced at Rachel as if deciding how much could be said.

"My only regret about Centrifugal Force has been what it did to you two. But I also had a feeling that the real problem had nothing to do with me, that there was something much deeper than jealousy at work, something that, for you, probably didn't even have much to do with Kane, except that it kept you from trusting what you had together. Was I wrong?"

"No," Rachel said with a wan smile. "You were very, very right."

Mariette let out a long sigh. "That's what I needed to know. What I've hated the worst about the whole situation was wondering if I was somehow at fault—"

"But you weren't," Rachel insisted, anxious to reassure. "It was all inside me. It was—"

Mariette held up a hand. "For now, the rest is between you and Kane."

Rachel couldn't suppress a pained chuckle. "That's another problem. The last I heard, we weren't speaking to each other."

Mariette shook her head. "How long's it going to last? Not another six years, I hope."

"Not if I can help it." Rachel's lips twisted wryly.

"Good." Mariette nodded, her smooth cap of pale hair catching moonlike gleams from the street lamp above. "Who knows," she mused, "you and I could possibly become...friends someday. When you're ready, you might even decide to design a party or two for me again."

In spite of herself, Rachel flinched. Did Mariette know about Louie Laird's plans for the party in October after all? "Forgive me," Mariette amended, aware of the sudden tension in Rachel. "Maybe I'm rushing things a little." The words were free of guile.

"Not really," Rachel said. "It's just that I think your new secretary is a few steps ahead of both of us."

"Louie? What's Louie got to do with . . ." Mariette's mouth dropped open as awareness dawned. "Oh, I think I begin to get the picture. Louie is out to make points with me by hooking me up with the best party designer in L.A., Illusions Unlimited."

Rachel nodded. "He's already called my assistant, Elaine, and asked for a proposal."

"Oh, Rachel. I'm sorry. If I'd known, I swear I never would have put you on the spot like that."

Rachel tipped her head to the side, considering. "I guess it's not Louie's fault if he wants the best for his new boss."

"No. No, of course not. But if you want me to . . ."

Rachel shrugged. "Why do anything? If it's all right with you, we'll just let our employees get on with their plans."

"It would simplify things," Mariette agreed cautiously.

"Then it's settled," Rachel said with finality. "Come on. Let's go inside."

Victoria was still somewhat subdued when they joined her in the house. Casting about for something to do while the time passed until Kane returned, Rachel suggested a game of Scrabble. She was happily surprised when the girl's eyes lit up. "I'm dynamite at Scrabble," Victoria announced with eager pride. "I'll beat the pants off both of you!"

Rachel brought out the board and tiles, and they played.

As it turned out, Vicky had not overestimated her talents. Rachel couldn't help wondering what the outcome would be if the girl were ever to match wits with Gran. The thought brought a smile to her lips. Perhaps someday she'd find out.

It was after eleven when the blue and white Buick pulled into the driveway. Kane got out and came up to the porch where Rachel waited with Mariette and Victoria.

His eyes raked over Rachel almost brutally before he spoke to Mariette. "The road is clear, and I can take you back to my place now."

Mariette nodded. "We can get Vicky's things and—"

"Go to bed," Kane said flatly.

"But Kane, I was hoping to—"

"Please don't argue with me, Mari. Mel would never forgive me if I let you take off in the middle of the night after a day like today."

"He's right, you know," Rachel added softly.

Mariette shrugged wearily. "I'll admit a nice firm mattress and a cup of hot milk sound very tempting at this particular moment."

Kane nodded in understanding. "Then let's go."

He looked exhausted, Rachel thought, the tiny lines beside his eyes etched more deeply than before.

"Thank you for the . . . guided tour, Rachel," Mariette was saying warmly. Rachel felt the other woman's hand firm in her own.

"Anytime. I mean that."

"I'm glad," Mariette replied, holding Rachel's gaze for long enough to communicate much more than the two short words implied. Then she was on her way down the porch steps.

"Umm . . . Rachel?" asked the crushed-velvet voice beside her.

Rachel bent to whisper in one delicate pink ear. "You're quite a woman, Victoria Sayer. I was very happy to have you in my grandmother's house. Don't forget what I said. About Kane's songs."

The violet eyes misted over for a moment. Then Victoria drew herself up to her full five feet four inches in heels. "I won't. Solemn vow."

"Solemn vow," Rachel echoed, smiling, as Victoria followed after her mother.

"I'll be back," Kane muttered cryptically.

"I know," Rachel answered, so low he couldn't have heard as he walked away.

THE BOTTLE OF LACRIMA CHRISTI Rachel had been saving was in a box on the service porch. She found an ancient corkscrew in a drawer and two juice glasses in a cupboard. She took Kane's guitar from where it waited by the couch and went out on the side porch.

Nat stretched out beside her as she sipped the earth-tasting wine. The primroses had opened hours ago, their glowing yellow blossoms like splashes of sunlight on the night. There was still the faintest hint of wood smoke on the air, testimony to the ever-present whims of nature.

For Rachel, alone, the time passed slowly. Still she remained on the side porch, strumming random chords on the guitar, her laughter at herself sweet and low when she realized she'd forgotten everything Kane had taught her.

She heard the car return, sliding almost silently into the driveway. There was the crunch of booted feet on gravel, muffled to a stalking whisper across the lawn.

And then the steady tread on the wooden steps. Rachel closed her eyes and leaned back.

When she opened them again there was a shadow in front of the sky. Kane.

"Nice of you to wait up for me."

"You're welcome." She smiled a lazy, catlike smile.

"Damn you, Rachel. I shouldn't forgive you. The things you said to me yesterday were—"

"Lies," she finished for him.

He flung himself down beside her. Nat licked his hand. "If this is an apology—" he began.

"It is."

"Will you stop interrupting me?"

"Sorry. Do you want a glass of wine?"

Rachel handed him the guitar. Kane laid it on the porch floor. She poured him a glass of wine and gave that to him, too. He took a swallow and set the glass by the guitar.

"I love you, Rachel," he said grimly. "Though God knows there have been times when I would have given anything not to. I tried for six years to forget you. But I guess I've always believed deep down that your ridiculous accusations about my nonexistent career as a stud service to all of Beverly Hills were just a—"

"An attempt to hide from the fact that I love you, as well."

He glared at her. "You're interrupting me again."

"You're absolutely right."

"About what?" he demanded with savage curiosity.

She studied the fiercely male landscape of his face, feeling the small frisson of desire and longing that always crept along her nerves at his nearness.

"Everything. It's true that I love you. I always have, I think. Since that second day in your aerobics class when you told me I was pushing too hard, and I snapped at you to shut up and do your job. I twisted my ankle right after that. Remember?"

Kane snorted grudgingly in answer.

Rachel laughed, a true laugh, full and bubbling up from deep within. "You think *you* would have given anything not to love *me*?" she teased. "Look at all the years I've wasted trying to run away from my love for you."

"But why?" The dark-timbred voice cut a wound of sound in the space between them.

When she answered Rachel found that the words flowed out quickly, tumbling over each other in their need to be said.

"It's all wrapped up in . . . my mother and my father. I thought you and I were the same. My last memory of my mother is of her screaming at him that she was leaving him, that she wanted her freedom.

"It was my tenth birthday. They had taken me to the zoo. It was my father's idea. An effort to pretend we were a normal family. But it was a serious miscalculation on his part. All the animals in cages. My mother hated it. She felt she was like them—trapped in a cage, with my father her keeper. I think those animals made her decide she was finally going to draw the line.

"We were returning to Catherine's. I was alone in the back seat, and they were arguing in front. She grabbed the wheel out of his hands. She was screaming that she was getting out now, and it was time for me to learn what would happen if I ever got stupid and fell for a man.

"The car shot off the road and slammed into a piling. At first I must have been knocked out. But I came to for a moment before the ambulance arrived. I called for them. They didn't answer.

"Can't you see? It got all twisted up inside me. The way they loved each other. It was poison for them. A battle for dominance rather than any kind of sharing. It wasn't only what you said the other morning, about love equaling loss. Losing them was terrible, but witnessing what they did to each other was much worse. Because even as a very small child, I could sense how desperately they loved each other and how impossible it was for them to find any common ground.

"Both my grandfathers had died before I was born. And both my grandmothers were strong, self-directed women who ran their own lives, alone. I wanted to be like my grandmothers, I *had* to be like my grandmothers. Or I was sure I'd end up like my mother. A caged, tortured thing, without a real self, a half person who had nothing but her keeper to define who she was.

"Oh, Kane. I *hurt* for her, for *them*. Because I know now that my father was just as caged in his own way. And then I met you. And you taught me . . . about passion. And I knew what I felt for you was as dangerous as what she felt for him. I thought it would be the same for us as for them. And I couldn't let that happen. So I . . . so I . . ." Her voice caught on a helpless sob.

Kane's strong arms came around her. She was held in a cradle of warm steel. "I loved you so, Kane. *Love* you so. I never knew how to tell you, couldn't bring myself to tell you. I thought loving you would mean I'd be less than myself. I couldn't believe it might make me more. So I fought it by telling myself lies about you."

Kane was rocking her gently, holding her fast. She could hear the crickets and the intermittent croaking of a solitary frog. From the dark secrecy of the moon-shadowed trees, the night birds cried plaintively, each to the other, soft reassurances that dawn would come at last.

A few minutes and a lifetime later, Rachel led Kane down through the garden to the wild rose bush that grew along the fence. She was conscious of the thorns when she found the tight new bud she wanted, but still one sharp point pierced her thumb. She didn't protest when Kane raised her hand to his mouth and took the liquid jewel into himself.

"You should be more careful." The subtle promise in the words was a near-physical caress. "The rose always exacts a price."

"It's worth it," she said with tender conviction.

"Your grandmother's garden is beautiful by moonlight. It almost seems . . . enchanted."

"My grandmother can grow anything." Rachel sighed and leaned into him, holding her face up like a flower to the sun. When his lips didn't meet hers, she pulled away enough to see what held him back.

"We were talking about prices. . . ."

"No, it was enchantment."

"Prices and terms," he said gruffly.

"Oh. That's right. The terms of your surrender." She drew the velvet tightness of the bud against the sandpaper cheek and down along the uncompromising line of his jaw. "But I thought I told you. It must be unconditional. I am very firm on this point."

"Does that mean I have to marry you?" he growled, the corners of his mouth betraying all his efforts to remain unmoved.

"Well." She brought the rose back to herself and breathed in the haunting, delicate scent. "That might be too much to demand, even of the utterly vanquished. A man who marries a woods witch would never get a moment's peace."

"You claimed unconditional surrender," he reminded her. "And I'm afraid now you're going to have to live with it." She tried to slither from his grasp, but he held her firm. "Will you marry me, Rachel?"

"I...never planned to get married." Her breath seemed suddenly barely enough to make the words come.

"Does that mean no?"

"It means I'm afraid." There. She had said it.

"Of me? Afraid I'll demand that you give up your career and produce two-point-two children the day after tomorrow?"

"No. Afraid I won't be any good at it. I know I'm brooding and hot-tempered. And I do have a tendency to jump to conclusions..."

"So we have at least three things in common."

"Oh, Kane. I'm serious."

"So am I. I don't promise it'll be easy, Rachel. That would be a lie. But damn it, I want the right to watch your golden face, all trusting while you sleep. To lie against your breasts and feel your heartbeat so I can match the steady sound to mine. To know when you sigh and pull me closer that your dreams are sweet and have me in them.

"I want that for every night of our lives. For that, I'll put up with how grouchy you are in the morning."

"Don't you own a comb?" She brushed the shock of hair back from his brow.

"Will you love me forever?"

"At least until Tuesday."

"Will you marry me, Rachel?"

"Yes. Oh, yes," she promised on a breath, so that only he and the night could hear.

His mouth was on hers then, in a conjuring caress. Rachel knew the spell they wove around each other was rising to claim them once again.

The lights of her grandmother's house shone brightly at the end of the garden path. Long ago, a girl child had lost the path in the night. It had taken a grown woman to find it again. She would follow it joyfully. It was the road home.

Harlequin Temptation

COMING NEXT MONTH

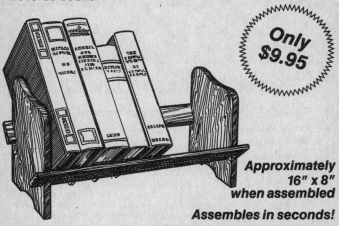

Take 4 best-selling love stories FREE
Plus get a FREE surprise gift!

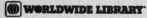

All men wanted her,
but only one man would have her.

Her cruel father had intended
Angie to marry a sinister cattle baron twice her age.
No one expected that she would fall in love with his
handsome, pleasure-loving cowboy son.

Theirs was a love no desert storm would quench.